JILTED

BISCAYNE BAY SERIES

BOOK 3

DEBORAH BROWN

JILTED
All Rights Reserved
Copyright © 2021 Deborah Brown

Cover: Natasha Brown

ISBN-13: 978-1-7334807-8-9

PRINTED IN THE UNITED STATES OF AMERICA

JILTED

Chapter One

A picture-perfect Florida day. Fluffy white clouds floated in the brilliant blue sky. The temperature hadn't warmed up enough to singe your skin off... yet. I contemplated my third cup of coffee, planning to take it out to the balcony and watch the waves lap the white sand of the southernmost tip of South Beach.

I barely made it off my stool at the kitchen island, steps from the coffee pot, when the front door flew open. I sighed and sat back down to wait, knowing it would only be seconds before the invaders made their appearance. I knew they couldn't be held off by my choice to ignore their incessant pounding. I'd better have a good reason to accompany my emphatic "No" to whatever they were planning. I leaned back and caught my two best friends, Harper Finn and Avery English, glancing around the living room/dining room before heading down the hall toward my bedroom. Not sure why they thought I'd still be in bed.

The three of us had met at the University of Miami and became fast friends, the friendship only getting stronger after graduation. Now we each owned a condo unit on the forty-first floor of a building I owned.

It took them less than a minute to figure out that they only had two locations left to check — the kitchen and the balcony. They barreled back down the hall and soon had me in their sights. I waved, checking out their colorful flowing spaghetti-strap sundresses, perfect for the Miami heat.

"Rella! You're just sitting there watching us look for you without saying a word?" Harper's tone conveyed that she wasn't quite sure whether to be upset or not. "I suggested that we kick your door down." She pointed to her strappy sandal. "Not the right kind of shoes, so I reluctantly decided to knock politely, and where did that get me? I know you heard us."

"I told Harper not to risk breaking her foot when I had a lockpick." Avery brandished one from her pocket. "You should be proud of your star pupil." She beamed at Harper, who'd taught her how to use it.

Harper had several sneaky tricks in her repertoire, none of them legal, and Avery wanted to learn every one of them. I had to admit that even I had learning them on my to-do list, but I hadn't made the time yet.

"The only practice I get is picking the locks at WD." Avery made a face.

Grey Walker and Seven Donnelly, Harper's and Avery's boyfriends, who'd partnered in opening WD Consulting, a private investigation firm, wouldn't be happy to hear that she picked their locks to hone her skills.

"And who listens to the endless grouching every time you do that, or any of your other sneaky tricks?" Harper pointed to herself. But if asked, she'd have to admit that she was the last to be opposed to a little drama. "I'm not sure where Grey got the idea that you were the fragile sort." She eyed Avery. "When he said that, I laughed at him and told him to tell you to knock it off."

"You need to stop with all the noise and banging on the door. What will the neighbors think? You two were loud enough for the residents on the floor below to hear," I said in a huff, knowing that the building was well-constructed and noises didn't travel; plus, we were the only residents on this floor. "You're lucky I didn't call the cops and report a break-in."

"Idle threat." Harper blew it off with a toss of her head and signaled to Avery. The two ran up to me, each grabbing an arm, and pulled me off the stool. "You're coming with us. Slip into a pair of those uncomfortable heels you love, and we'll get out of here."

My Saint Bernard, Bruno, who'd been lying at my feet, didn't bat an eyelash at their manhandling or the fact that I'd barely managed to step over his massive body without landing on him.

I looked down at my silk ankle pants and bare manicured feet. Out of habit, I always dressed as though at any minute, weekend or not, the office would call and I'd drop everything to go in. Too many times, I went with the thought that I'd only stay for a few minutes, but it always turned into hours. I knew that if I went to the office today, it would be one of those days. "I can't. I need to check in at the office after being away, and I've got a file on my desk that needs my immediate attention." Okay, lame excuse. Even they knew there was no reason to go in on the weekend except for my obsessive need for control.

The Cabot Foundation was started by my parents. After they died when their private plane went down, I stepped in as CEO and poured my energy into helping women's and children's charities. I was determined that it would continue to be a success, even if it meant long hours.

"Fibber," Avery said, hands on her hips. "You're too young to be married to your job." I wondered if she noticed me flinch. "Saturday breakfast is a ritual. You've already missed one week for that wedding in the Bahamas, and we've yet to hear details. I'm betting that nothing earth-shattering happened at the foundation while you were gone and anything you need to do will still be there tomorrow."

"We're not going to take no for an answer," Harper said, a finger-shake in her tone.

"Can't we—"

"No excuses," Harper cut me off. "If you force us, we *will* drag you out of here, and then how will *the* Rella Cabot explain being barefoot?" She made an expression of faux shock.

"I'm taking my own car," I yelled as I headed down the hallway toward my bedroom.

"And give us the slip? Don't think so," Avery yelled back.

We know each other so well. I laughed, having thought of doing just that. I slid into a pair of my favorite heels, ran a brush through my shoulder-length blond hair, and grabbed my purse. How was I going to tell them? I knew it'd have to be sooner or later, but I was really pushing for later. Much later. I met them at the front door, and they both laughed, thoroughly amused with themselves for pulling off their coup.

The three of us chatted as we rode down in the elevator to the garage and climbed into Harper's SUV.

It was a short drive to the Cat House Café on Washington Boulevard, and as usual, there were a dozen people lined up on one side of the front patio, a few spilling out onto the sidewalk. All of the outside tables were filled, which meant that the inside would be crowded as well.

Today, the owner, Prissy Mayes, was manning the front door, greeting guests, and she waved us right in. She was rocking an ankle-length fuchsia boho tunic dress, an army of bracelets up both arms, and her signature look, a flower—this one a gardenia—clipped in her bright-red hair.

I had a few personal projects of my own that I backed, and this restaurant was one of my favorites. I'd invested in it, loving the addition that had been built onto the back patio—an enclosed area that acted as a playroom for cats available for adoption. I exchanged cheek kisses with Prissy.

"Business is great," she whispered in my ear.

"As evidenced by the line I see out front every time I drive by." I smiled back.

Prissy escorted us to our regular corner table on the back patio, which faced the glassed-in room for the cats. The kittens were active today, running up and down the scratching posts and leaping back and forth. There were two older cats cuddled up together, asleep in one of the overstuffed chairs.

Harper stopped at the bar on the way in and ordered a round of mimosas, which arrived not long after we sat down. "Best friends," she toasted. We raised our glasses.

"We've barely seen you since you got back from the wedding last weekend." Avery made a sad face. "Tell us that you didn't have a terrible time."

One of my biggest donors, Marcella, had been invited to the wedding of a friend of hers in the

Bahamas and needed a plus one. It did sound fun when she first pitched the idea, and I didn't blame her for not wanting to go by herself. "It was hectic, and the time flew by." I felt my cheeks grow warm, more than a few memories vivid in my mind. "You two insisted that I have a good time, and I did. The warm waters rival ours here in Florida." I downed the rest of my mimosa, wanting another.

"We're eager for the details." Harper held up her hand, silently ordering another round of drinks.

Mind reader. I smiled.

"Better yet, did you manage to take pictures?" Avery asked, excited to see whatever I'd snapped.

I didn't want to break it to her that the thought never occurred to me.

"The wedding…"

A breeze blew across the water and cooled down the day. The sun was setting, and fingers of color splashed across the sky. They were still bright but would soon fade, settling into dark-blue tones as it turned to night.

Marcella and I were among the first guests to arrive. All the seating was on one side of the aisle, and we were shown to seats in the second row of chairs in front of the flower-draped altar, within feet of where the blue-green water lapped the shore. The rest of the guests trickled in by ones and twos and made their way down the wooden walkway over the white sand. The crowd turned out to be small and intimate, all smiling and a number of them barefoot.

A woman seated herself at the baby grand piano and started playing. At the same time, fireworks shot into the air, bursting overhead and showering the sky with bright flashes of color.

The first to make an appearance was the groom, a well-dressed thirty-something, his black hair slicked back, in well-tailored white slacks and a dress shirt with a white rose pinned to it. Behind him was his best man, dressed the same except he wore a red rose. They moved up the petal-strewn aisle to where the pastor stood, their friends calling out greetings.

The groom-to-be and best man turned and stared down the aisle. They leaned towards each other, and the best man said something that made them both laugh. Then they waited. And waited.

It was at least fifteen minutes before a woman in a strapless sea-green dress came down the aisle and stopped in front of the groom, the best man stepping to his side. It was a short conversation, and then she left, an uncomfortable smile on her face. The groom talked to the pastor, who patted him on the shoulder.

Taking the microphone, the groom turned to the assembled guests. You could have heard a pin drop. "My bride has changed her mind, and there won't be a wedding. I want to thank all of you for coming. There's an open bar and plenty to eat."

"What?" Harper and Avery shrieked.

"Wasn't Marcella friends with the bride? What did she say?" Harper demanded.

"Marcella…" I laughed. "Realizing that the groom, Pryce Thornton, was now a free man, she ran after him with a proposal of her own. Her parting words to me were, 'I'll offer my condolences and my phone number.' By then, I needed a drink and went to the beach bar."

"I'm assuming the woman who broke the news wasn't the bride-to-be?" Avery asked, and Harper nodded, also wanting to know. "How awful, and to wait until the groom was already at the altar…"

"I ended up mingling with a few of Pryce's friends at the bar and found out that the woman who broke the news was a friend of the bride and the maid of honor," I said. "They talked about placing a bet about whether she'd volunteered to be the bearer of the news, but no one knew her well enough to ask."

"You partied with the groom's friends?" Harper asked, sounding excited.

"Before you start with a hundred questions, 'partied' is grossly overstating it. What I did was order a drink, sip slowly, and listen to their conversations. The consensus was 'Good riddance.' And before one of you asks—because I know what's coming next—no, I never met the bride or any of her other friends. Just a brief glance at the one who delivered the 'It's off,' message. Not sure what I would've said after the usual pleasantries, had I been introduced. I'm not very pushy when it comes to things that are none of my business. And to answer your next question, the groom didn't come to the party."

"Then you smiled politely, went back to your room, and read a book," Avery said with a knowing nod.

I shot them both a glare. "I'll have you know, I got another drink and walked along the shoreline. Ran into this gorgeous stranger, and well... we hooked up." *So there* in my tone.

They both gasped.

Not entirely true—he wasn't a complete stranger, as I *did* recognize him, though we hadn't been formally introduced. "We spent the rest of the weekend together."

Not sure who laughed first, but they were both laughing, neither believing a word.

"When have you ever known me to lie? Or even engage in half-truths? Unless it's for a favor I'm doing for one of you." I maintained eye contact ·with them, not flinching. "You two are always encouraging me to do something a bit wild, and when I do, you stare at me like I made everything up. Now that's annoying."

It took them a minute, but they both came around to believing me.

"Details." Avery snapped her fingers. Harper grinned. "You're smiling, which is good and can only mean you had a good time. Like a really good one." She tapped her finger impatiently on the tabletop. "Name, social security number, and I'll run a background check on the man." Avery, an established financial consultant, had ventured off into doing background investigations and now split her time between finance and investigation, working exclusively for WD on the latter.

"I'll admit that he and I may have tipped a few—an open bar is hard to resist. A drink or two, and we ended up spending the rest of the weekend on a yacht, talking about everything and nothing."

They both shrieked.

"Keep your voices down before we get kicked out." I tossed a glance over my shoulder. "People are staring." I froze in my chair, looking up into familiar deep-blue eyes.

"Are you going to introduce your husband to your friends?"

Chapter Two

"You're what?" Harper and Avery squealed in unison.

Now everyone in the restaurant had stopped eating and was staring at our table.

Those blue eyes held my attention. "I'm getting an annulment," I whispered. There was no way it could be Pryce Thornton in the flesh—the man I'd spent the weekend with... and married—and yet here he was, smiling down at me.

Pryce swooped in and laid a big kiss on me. "No, you are not," his familiar voice grouched. "We don't meet the requirements for an annulment." Although he'd lowered his voice, my friends heard and stared in shocked amusement.

Grey and Seven were behind him, both wearing big smirks. Seven dragged over three more chairs, and the men sat down, Pryce next to me. Grey made the introductions.

A waiter appeared with a bottle of champagne and a tray of glasses, setting one in front of each of us.

"To the newlyweds," Grey toasted.

Pryce pulled me close, planting a kiss on my cheek. "I'm a very lucky man."

All of us clinked glasses, including me, though I'd been caught off guard and was still struggling for what to say, and at the same time trying to figure out my feelings beyond the excitement of seeing the man again. I realized that I'd missed him.

"Grey and I thought, what a great way to share the happy news?" Seven said with a grin.

"We're the last to know!" Harper exclaimed.

Avery apparently didn't feel the least bit slighted, as she could barely sit still, hopping with excitement.

"You can't imagine my surprise…" Grey gave us an exaggerated look of disbelief, swallowing laughter. "Or maybe you can. Got a call this morning from my old friend Pryce, who needed help locating his missing wife, Rella Cabot. Even better, he was in the area on business. Turned out to be the easiest job ever, since I knew right where to find the missing bride."

"When were you planning on telling us that you married the jilted groom?" Avery smirked, joining Harper in checking Pryce out.

I'd wanted to tell my friends but didn't know how to drop the bombshell that I'd gotten married. And to someone I'd only just met. I put off answering, instead turning and locking eyes with Pryce. "How did you…?" I'd left him a note that I'd be getting an annulment and snuck off, catching an early flight. I'd been home several days but found one excuse or another not to contact my lawyer.

"Find my errant bride?" Pryce finished my question, brushing a kiss on my cheek. "Imagine my surprise at waking up and no wife. So we're clear, I think we should give this marriage a shot. Our time in the Bahamas, while short, was idyllic, and we found out early on that we were perfect for one another, wouldn't you agree?"

My cheeks burned, and I couldn't bring myself to look at my friends. After all, I was the responsible one of the threesome.

"Lucky me, the sea captain that married us was still dockside, and I was able to track him down and get a copy of the marriage license, though it didn't have as much information as I'd hoped for."

"Married on a yacht? So romantic," Avery gushed.

"It was very fast... We barely know one another," I reminded Pryce, leaving unsaid that a few drinks were involved.

"What better way for us to learn everything there is to know about each other than by working on our marriage? I'm looking forward to every day we spend together. Say yes." Pryce kissed the back of my hand.

I wasn't sure if it was Avery or Harper that sighed... or both.

"Before these two expire from excitement over

Pryce romancing Rella..." Seven nodded at Avery and Harper. "How about another toast?" He refilled our glasses. "To the new couple."

Pryce hooked his arm around me and held me close, and we all drank our champagne.

"I'll go first," Avery said in an excited tone.

I groaned inwardly and nudged her under the table, which she ignored.

"The bride, the first one anyway, ditches you... at the altar, no less—isn't that a dude thing to do?" Avery asked.

"Honey." Seven bumped her shoulder with his.

"Not to throw you under the bus..." I squeezed Pryce's hand. "But if you don't answer at least one question, they'll grill me, and I'll spill everything I know to get them to stop."

Pryce winked at me, not the least bit put off. "Things started to go south shortly after my bride, Lili, and I got down to the island. The next day, she boasted to everyone at the bridal luncheon that she'd done a good job of choosing a man with lots of money for her to spend. Then went on to advise a newly engaged friend to run a financial check on her intended groom before tying the knot."

Harper's and Avery's mouths dropped open. It was all I could do not to emulate them. I'd known that part of Pryce and Lili's problems had to do with money, and heard some of the details, but I hadn't asked questions.

Harper leaned forward and asked Pryce, "How did you find out?"

"Katie, my best man's wife, was also in attendance and decided to test Lili's reaction to telling her Pryce recently took a major loss, saying that he'd recover, but it might take a couple of years. According to her, Lili bemoaned, 'I never agreed to marry a poor man.'"

"Awkward." Harper made a face. "And to someone she knew was a friend of yours. Or her husband was anyway."

"As soon as the lunch was over, Katie got on the phone to her husband, Mike, still livid about how Lili talked about me only in terms of my bank balance. Mike, who's been a friend forever, called me right away. While I was trying to digest everything, he insisted that I had to let it play out to know for sure if Lili was only tying the knot for money and if she confronted me about Katie's 'revelation,' I had to go along with the story." Pryce finished off his drink. "I wanted to sit down with Lili right away but went along with Mike's suggestion. It took another day before she came to me about what Katie had said. I told her not to worry, that although we'd have to cut back for a while, we'd eventually get back on solid financial footing."

"How did she respond?" Harper asked.

"It was clear she was shocked. After an uncomfortable silence, she said all the right words, very understanding, and assured me that we'd get through it together," Pryce said. "Her words and facial expression were at odds, and I fully expected her to tell me the wedding was off. Honestly, it would've been fine with me, as I was beginning to wonder if my bride had any real feelings for me at all."

"At that point, when was the wedding taking place?" Grey asked.

"Next day. Even though tradition says that the bride and groom don't see one another before the ceremony, Lili called early and demanded that we meet on the beach. I figured she was ending everything."

The server stopped by, wanting to know if he could refill drinks. I'd had enough champagne and ordered orange juice, and the rest all ordered something different.

"You can't leave us hanging," Avery said.

Pryce laughed, not put off by her nosiness. "The two of us ended up down at the shoreline, where Lili unloaded on me about keeping secrets and rambled on about things that made no sense. I was about ready to suck it up and tell her it wasn't going to work out when she launched into hysterics. I calmed her down, and after drying her eyes on my shirt, she said, 'Thanks for comforting me. We're going to make this work. See you later,' then turned and sprinted back up the beach."

"What did you decide to do next?" Seven asked.

"I went for a run, during which I convinced myself it was nothing more than a case of nerves, and decided to track Lili down and make sure that marriage was what we both wanted. Couldn't find her anywhere. Looking back, I think she may have left the resort. It didn't occur to me that she'd leave me at the altar; I wouldn't have done it to her, despite feeling unsure." Pryce picked up his water glass and downed half. "The last thing I expected was for her to be a no-show… My friends were ecstatic, since after they heard about the lunch, they didn't like her. Needing to get away from everyone, I started down the beach and ran into this woman, who swept me off my feet and changed my life. I know it was rushed and we didn't think out every detail, but I don't have a single regret." He brought my knuckles to his lips and kissed them.

My cheeks continued to blaze with heat as I stared into his eyes and he stared back.

"Did you two get all your questions answered?" Grey directed to Harper and Avery. "Good," he said, not giving either one a chance to answer.

"Where's Bruno?" Pryce eyed the area around the table. "I thought you took him everywhere?"

"You know about Rella's dog?" Avery asked, surprise in her tone.

"We shared a few secrets." Pryce winked at me. "I'm looking forward to meeting Bruno. And I'm hoping he doesn't eat me."

I laughed since Bruno was a sweetheart and would love having a new playmate.

Harper turned to Grey. "You said that you and Pryce were friends?"

"We met in college, became fast friends, partied it up, and chased girls." Grey laughed at the memories. "Afterwards, we kept in sporadic touch, as we'd gone in different directions. Me into law enforcement, while Pryce, a numbers freak like Avery, joined an investment firm before striking out on his own. That's why he got in touch—he was thinking I was still a cop and wanted a recommendation for a private investigator. Told him he was in luck and went on to tell him about the business Seven and I started. Once I heard his story, I wasn't missing a second of the reunion. I filled Seven in, and he also wanted a ringside seat."

"You two staying married or what?" Avery asked.

"I vote an emphatic yes." Pryce winked. "We're compatible in a lot of ways."

"We need *private* time to talk." I patted his hand and glared at Avery to stop.

"Or you two could date," Harper said, liking her idea. "Get to know one another better." She nodded, liking whatever ideas were whirling around in her brain.

"I'm thinking we can come to a mutually agreeable arrangement." Pryce grinned. "I don't know how I got so lucky, being on the beach that night, but I've decided that it was fated."

Harper and Avery oohed and awed.

"We've got a couple of *fated* stories for you right here at this table," Seven said, and he and Grey laughed.

Suddenly, the restaurant went silent. As we looked around, trying to determine the reason, Miami cops surrounded the table—four in total.

"Pryce Thornton?" the lead cop asked. Pryce nodded. "You need to stand. Hands behind your back. You're under arrest for the murder of Liliana Ford."

"Murder?" Pryce and I gasped simultaneously.

"I didn't—" he started.

"You have the right to remain silent…" the cop continued.

"You have a lawyer?" Avery asked. Pryce shook his head. "I've got the best on speed dial—Cruz Campion." Two of the cops looked at her in surprise. "Not one word until Cruz gets to the station. He doesn't like it when you talk without him present."

"Don't worry, pal. We've got your back," Grey assured Pryce.

Just that fast, he was cuffed and marched out.

Prissy rushed over, her bracelets jiggling up and down her arms. "So sorry about your friend, but once word gets out, I'll be busier than ever. This is already a popular table; I may have to charge a premium."

Floridians loved drama and never got tired of it. In fact, bring it on.

"That's Rella's new husband, Pryce Thornton," Harper told Prissy.

"Congrats." Prissy bent down and swept me into a hug. "I'm sure that whatever the problem is, they have the wrong man and he'll be coming home to you soon." She patted my shoulder.

"I need to... uh." I grabbed my purse, about to stand, when Seven covered my hand with his.

Avery whipped her phone out and scrolled across the screen, then made a call. "Hey Cruzer, I've got a client for you. Name's Pryce Thornton. Being hauled off as we speak. No worries, I told him to keep his trap shut until you got to the station." Whatever he said, she giggled. "I'm thinking he's not guilty, but could be wrong." More giggles. "I'll tell him. You're a sweetheart." She hung up. "Cruz sends his felicitations."

"I'll bet," Seven mumbled. "Cruzer, huh?" He shook his head. "How the hell did you get his private number? You snooping through my phone again?"

"The man can have more than just you as a friend, Mr. Surly. I gave him investment advice. It made him a few bucks, which made him happy, and he forked over his number with an admonition not to call unless it was important." Avery smirked at Seven.

"What do I do?" I asked.

"First off, take a deep breath." Seven moved

closer, putting his arm around me. "Then you wait for a call from Cruz. I can guarantee that he'll keep you informed, and I'm certain he'll call as soon as he's done talking to Pryce."

"You'll need to be patient," Grey said. "It generally takes a few days to get before a judge for a bail hearing. In the meantime, I'll call in a couple of favors and get you a jail visit, if you'd like to go see him."

I nodded.

"No worries about getting a good bail bondsman. I've got a reputable one," Avery offered and, at Seven's and Grey's quizzical stares, added, "I didn't pinch yours; I got one of my own."

"It makes no sense that Pryce would murder Lili, not when he was relieved she left him at the altar," I said.

"Agreed." Grey nodded. "I've known Pryce a long time, and he's no murderer."

"I know this is overwhelming. What will make it tolerable is that Cruz, Grey, and I will keep you up to date with everything that's happening," Seven assured me.

Chapter Three

Pryce stayed behind bars for three weeks, the first bail hearing having been delayed. Although Seven got me several visits, we were warned not to talk about the case, and by silent agreement, we decided to include discussion of anything personal in the list, as all visits were recorded. I didn't ask if he murdered Lili—I knew he didn't do it. He tried to reassure me that life behind bars wasn't so bad, but the dark circles under his eyes told a different story.

I was relieved when Cruz's office called to inform me that the new bail hearing had been calendared for the morning session, and everything had gone as he predicted, right down to the amount of the bail. I'd offered to post it myself, but Pryce had it covered. Cruz had forbidden me to show up for the bail hearing— said it wouldn't look good to have the new wife at a hearing about the murder of the ex-fiancée— but I'd be damned if I wouldn't at least pick Pryce up. I chose ankle pants, a silk top, and a pair of flats—one of the few times I ignored my stilettos—raced down to my SUV, and easily cruised over to the Miami jail.

The waiting room was a large open space with windows on one side and a long reception counter on the far wall. I approached the desk and waited patiently while the woman finished whatever she was doing and acknowledged me. "Do you know when Pryce Thornton will be released?"

"That door over there—" She pointed across the room. "—you'll know when he walks through it. Have a seat."

I chose a chair that didn't have anyone sitting on either side and had a clear view of the door. The sturdy plastic seat was as uncomfortable as it looked. I wanted to put on my dark glasses so I could check out the room without being spotted but thought that would attract attention and get me labeled shady. I glanced about furtively—more than half the chairs were full, and all the occupiers were minding their own business. I'd brought in my phone for entertainment after double-checking the rules to make sure it wasn't a violation. Cruz warned me when he called that Pryce's release could take hours, but I'd still raced over, wanting to be here when he walked out. I scrolled aimlessly, my attention focused on the door, which opened with regularity, hoping that the next one out would be Pryce. One thing those getting released had in common—they all hustled to get outside. Most had someone there to meet them, but a couple of the men didn't, and they didn't make eye contact with anyone as they beelined for the exit. As soon as the chairs around me emptied, they filled up again.

The door opened once again. This time, Pryce walked out, looking more worn than when I saw him last. I jumped up and ran to meet him. His arms circled me, and he hugged me hard, grumbling in my ear, "Very happy to see you. Let's get the hell out of here." He slung his arm around my shoulders, and I pointed the way to where I parked.

At the car, he opened the driver's door for me and bent down to kiss me before going around to the other side. "I can't believe that you didn't ditch me and run for the beach." He leaned over the console and kissed me again.

"I'll admit to being conflicted. I'm the one who overthinks everything, and yet I jumped into marriage, of all things, without a second thought. One side of me thinks we have things in common, so why not explore them? After all, we *are* married. The other side thinks I'm nuts."

"I was thinking along the same lines." Pryce laughed, then sobered. "There's something I want you to know. I didn't—"

I put my finger across his lips. He kissed my fingertips. "I already know what you're going to say, and I never thought for one second that you killed Lili."

Pryce wrapped his hand around mine.

I shot out of the parking lot and weaved my way through traffic, hoping I never had a reason to come back.

"I want to thank you for using your connections for me. Cruz told me right off that he was a damn good lawyer, but he somehow inspired confidence instead of coming across as though he was trying to pull some con." Pryce chuckled. "He out-lawyered the prosecution, for which I was grateful."

"I would've posted the bail—did it once before, and it's easy." I shot him a quick smile. "As for the visits, the jail perks, and the rest, that was all Grey and Seven. Being ex-cops, it seems like they know everyone, and both still have friends on the force, especially Seven."

"Your visits meant everything. They kept me sane."

"You might not know, but Cruz and Seven are longtime friends and when Avery was charged with a murder she didn't commit, Cruz was the one Seven called." I nodded at his raised eyebrows. "And look, she's on the loose." He chuckled. "Avery's a big Cruz fan. Told us that it's because he's full of himself and doesn't mind flaunting it. Between you and me, I think she'd like to learn how to do that herself. People have a tendency to read her off-the-charts IQ as stupidity. Harper and I have told her on numerous occasions that they're lame."

"Watching Cruz at work made me a believer. Happy that he got me bail, which I considered a longshot."

"Just about everyone's getting bail these days," I said, even though I'd also thought it was a longshot and was just happy he was out.

"Also relieved that your friends didn't talk you into getting rid of me, and fast."

"Wait until you hear how Harper and Avery hooked up with their significant others." I chuckled. "One involved kidnapping, but I'll let them tell the story." I wasn't certain he believed me, but once he heard their tales, he'd know that we fit right in as a couple.

"So you know, I have an appointment with Mr. Campion, please call me Cruz, in the morning. A sit-down to discuss what to expect going forward." Pryce let out a long sigh. "Only a few minutes into our first meeting at the jail, I became convinced that if anyone could get me a not-guilty verdict, it would be him, but still, innocent people do go to prison."

"That's not going to happen to you." I was getting close to the Causeway and wanted to power down the windows and drink in the sea breeze that skimmed over the blue waters.

"I hate to keep asking for favors, but I need to pick up my car. Then go home and grab some clothes. I'd love it if you would make the drive to Palm Beach with me."

I told him on one of the jail visits that I expected him to stay with me once he got out—"My house is more centrally located, closer to your attorney and the courthouse." —and was happy when he agreed. "It's covered." I smiled at his look of surprise. "Your SUV is parked in the garage of the building where the five of us live. In addition to being a successful financial consultant, Avery's a talented PI and quickly tracked down one of your partners—Wesley Matthews. It turned out that Grey also knows the man, who made arrangements for several changes of clothes to be delivered. The two have stayed in touch with updates. You also have great friends." I winked at him.

"My partners must be flipping over the news that I was arrested, since I'm certain it garnered a headline or two—'Venture Capitalist charged with murder.' Hope my problems aren't going to smear the business we've built."

"This is Florida. Scandal's always good for business. If you were single, the women would be sending their resumes."

"What about your reputation?" Pryce asked in a tone conveying that he was more worried about me than him.

"Not to worry there either, as my friends aren't going anywhere." I squeezed his hand as I merged onto the Causeway and headed toward South Beach, the water that flowed along both sides of the highway bluer and more vibrant than usual.

Pryce fished his keys out of his pocket and held them up. "How exactly was my car moved?"

"You know those connections you were lauding me for? Well, one is handy with a slim jim, and that same person hotwired your car. Since I went along, I know there was a heated discussion about who was going to do the job. It got solved with no bloodshed." I grinned at his raised eyebrows.

"I know generally where we're headed, having been over this Causeway a few times and liking the drive, and hope that's a clue to our destination."

I wanted to laugh at the realization that Pryce wasn't certain if the offer I'd made to stay with me was serious. That was a couple of weeks ago, and it hadn't come up again. I knew he was going to like what I had in mind. I did, once I got used to the boldness of the idea. "Hint: there's lots of room and no bars on the windows."

"Jail humor." He wrinkled his nose. "Which there was little of—pretty much minded my own business."

"You know, I talked to Wesley a couple of times," I said to change the subject. I'd seen him at the wedding but hadn't been introduced. "He had questions about me that Grey didn't feel comfortable answering. Plus, Grey knew very little of how we met and our nuptials and thought I should be the one to answer those questions anyway. I still haven't confided everything to my friends. I've gotten a pass because of the whole arrest drama, but I expect that to come to an end now and I'll get a grilling." I chuckled.

"I imagine Wesley thought I'd lost my mind. Knowing him, he had a ton of questions."

"It's nice to have friends who care about you. He was annoyed that he hadn't heard the news from you and instead learned about it from a headline. After he recovered from that shock, he wanted to make sure I wasn't some gold digger. During our first conversation, I gave him my full name and told him to run a check. In the ensuing calls, there were no more questions about my money-grubby intentions." I'd done my best to win Wesley over on the phone by being candid and honest. "We ended up having a few laughs. I told him I'd pass it along that the next time you get married, you're required to let him know ahead of time."

"I'm surprised that none of them visited."

"Wesley told me that he tried, but you have to book in advance unless you have connections. He didn't ask how I was able to make it happen, and I didn't elaborate, not wanting to get Seven in trouble. I planned to meet him when he dropped off your clothes but had a meeting that I couldn't get out of. I asked Avery to stand in; she and Wesley talked, and she reported that the meeting went great. Knowing her, she had plenty of questions and talked his ear off." I exited the highway and turned toward the southern tip of Miami Beach.

"I have a bunch of calls to make, and he'll be first on the list. If I don't go to the big house, we're going to make this work."

"All things considered, you take a good booking photo," I said to lighten the mood.

"It's quite the process." He shook his head. "They don't ask what you think of the photos; they just steer you on to the next step."

"Heads up: Avery ran a background check on you. No good dirt, by the way."

"This is my first and hopefully last arrest." Pryce stared out the window at boats passing by on the bay as I maneuvered the streets. "The water is spectacular down here. I love everything about the beach. The view never gets old."

"Something else we have in common. You're going to like the miles of white sand down here, though I imagine you have that at your house too."

"I don't get there as often as I'd like."

Another turn, and I pulled into the underground parking garage of the high rise where I lived. Only a handful of people knew I lived in the penthouse. Even fewer knew I owned the building. I parked next to Pryce's car.

"You live in a hotel?" he joked.

"Forty-two floors of condos. A few are owned, but most are rentals."

Chapter Four

Taking out my security card, I inserted it into the card reader and got us into the lobby, then pointed to the farthest of the two elevators, where I used it again. "This elevator only goes to the top floor." I hit the only button on the panel. "We're at the southern end of South Beach and have a spectacular view of Biscayne Bay. There's nothing like it around," I said on the ride up.

Pryce turned me towards him so we were face to face. "You wouldn't let me say this before, but I want there to be no doubt—I did not kill Lili. In fact, I never even thought about it. Nor have I ever given thought to offing anyone."

"If I had the slightest doubt, I'd have let your friend Wesley pick you up."

"We need to talk about where we go from here. This could be a long, drawn-out ordeal. Not to mention the ramifications of being associated with an accused murderer." Pryce winced.

"Stop. You need to catch your breath, and I bet a long, hot shower will feel good." The doors opened, I grabbed his hand, and we stepped out. "You've met my neighbors—the first door is Avery and Seven's unit. The farthest one is

32

Harper and Grey's." I pointed to the opposite end of the hall. "The girls stop by whenever the mood strikes, and they never knock, so keep covered." I unlocked my door and ushered him inside.

The entry opened into a large, wide-open space that encompassed the living room and dining room, with the kitchen off to one side. Glass pocket doors ran the length of the room, opening out onto the balcony, with a view of the beach down below.

Pryce pulled me into his arms and kissed me.

The front door flew open, and Pryce and I broke apart.

"Oops, we're interrupting," Avery said, sounding happy that she'd caught us. Harper was right behind, straining to see around her, not wanting to miss anything.

"This is what I just warned you about," I said, laughing. "Although I *hoped* we'd have a few minutes of privacy." I arched a brow at the two women.

Pryce turned to face Avery and Harper, who weren't the least bit embarrassed. "No worries. I'm certain I can remember what we were doing when we were *interrupted*."

"Which security feed were you monitoring?" I asked Avery. "She's a snooper and will know your pants size shortly, if she doesn't already," I told Pryce, who didn't appear to believe me but would find out.

Now there was a knock at the door.

"You might as well let your boyfriends in." I quirked my head at Avery and Harper. "They knock," I whispered to Pryce, though Avery heard and wrinkled her nose.

Harper backed up and opened the door, holding it open as Grey and Seven walked in, smirks on their faces.

"Welcome back from the pen." Grey clapped Pryce on the shoulder. "You don't appear all that bedraggled, considering how long you were a guest of the county."

Connections helped him get out on bail or he'd still be there. I stepped closer and put my hand on his lower back.

"My first meeting with Cruz, he told me to keep my head down and mind my own business, and I followed that advice." Pryce grimaced. "Some didn't and only created problems for themselves."

"We're at maximum capacity for my entry." I motioned for everyone to follow me and led them out onto the balcony, where there was a large dining table on one side with plenty of seating. There was a separate door into the kitchen, which I opened. "What do you want to drink? I've got a refrigerator full of a little of everything."

Harper stepped up. "I've got this," she said and stepped around me. I winked at her in appreciation. She was back out quickly with a tray and served us all.

"Before you do anything, you need to get a background check on Hottie, in case he's a perv." Harper set a beer down in front of Pryce.

"Too late. Avery jumped on that one and got it to me within a day," I said with a laugh. "She didn't dig up any good dirt." I made a face at Pryce, who laughed.

"You're a catch, babes," Avery said to me, eyes wide. "Had to make sure he wasn't some unsavory sort. I also ran a credit report—great score and no issues."

Grey and Seven laughed, a *you're on your own, buddy* look on their faces.

"If it would put your fears to rest, I'm happy to have a postnup drawn up," Pryce told Avery. "What's Rella's stays Rella's."

"That must mean that quickie divorce is off the table." Harper looked to me for confirmation. I shook my head, telegraphing *behave*. "Before your marriage was outed in a headline, I was thinking of ways to repair Rella's reputation, should it need it, since yours is in the toilet and I didn't want it to reflect on her," she said, as though Pryce didn't know. "That option is now off the table, since some reporter got a copy of the marriage certificate and published it. You two are the latest fodder in the gossip section. If approached, my advice is to smile, even if you think the person needs their butt kicked."

"Harper's the social media queen," I told

Pryce. "Owns Finn Media and stays on top of everything for her clients."

"Why did I think you two were private investigators?" Pryce asked Harper and Avery, who both looked pleased at the assumption.

"Neither one is licensed." Seven gave the two women an even stare. "That doesn't mean they'd turn down an opportunity to stick their noses in... so beware."

"I did warn him," I said, ignoring the glares from Harper and Avery.

"Hey!" Avery grouched but looked ready to laugh. "Everyone at this table knows I do a good job."

I nodded, knowing how thorough she prided herself on being.

"If you weren't so damn good, we wouldn't have hired you to do background checks for the office," Grey told her. "Another perk is that she turns them around faster than anyone we've used in the past."

"You're leaving out that Avery initially muscled her way through the door with the help of her lockpick, and then refused to leave." Seven laughed at her.

"As everyone knows, and Pryce will find out, if I don't keep busy, trouble finds me," Avery said.

"Are you the one that jacked my car?" Pryce asked her.

"I was not." Her eyes shot to Harper.

"You just outed me," Harper grouched at her.

"I'm still annoyed at you. You knew I wanted to practice with the slim jim, but no, you had to do it all yourself. And mumbling 'we don't have all day' was just mean."

Seven wrapped his arms around Avery and kissed the top of her head. "You can jack my car any time."

"You've probably realized by now that you hooked up with the boring one in the group," I said to Pryce.

He leaned in and brushed his lips with mine. "You could never be a bore."

"Once, we were all goodie two-shoes; can't say I miss those days," Harper said with a shake of her head. "Now I'd say that we're not afraid to think outside the box."

Avery pulled a thumb drive out of her pocket and set it down in front of Pryce. "I ran a background check on Lili and her family."

"Are you certain that whoever you found is related?" Pryce asked, a look of disbelief on his face. "Lili told me that her mother died in a car accident years ago, refused to talk about her father, and said that she was an only child."

"When you get to know me, you'll find out that I double-check everything," Avery said. "Both her mother and brother are alive and well. The mother, Doris Ford, lives on the outskirts of Miami in a not-so-nice area. Maybe it was easier to say that she died than explain why they didn't have a relationship. It's also possible that Lili didn't want you finding out about her mother's rap sheet—an assortment of financial crimes: bad checks, theft, and one charge that involved a con to hustle an old guy out of cash. The charges were eventually dropped, but that's only because the man packed his truck and didn't leave a forwarding."

"And the brother?" I asked.

"Reed Ford has no criminal record and a clean credit report, and that's because he doesn't have any. Not a single credit card. There were a couple of addresses listed, but who knows if they're still good."

"I combed through Lili's social media accounts, and they showed her to be a partier," Harper told us. "One post after another of her having a good time, always in the middle of the action. Somehow, though, there wasn't word one about being engaged."

Pryce turned his attention to Grey and Seven. "Someone wanted Lili dead, and I'm hiring the two of you to find out anything you can."

"Why those two? What about me?" Avery huffed in indignation.

I bit back a smile, waiting to see how Pryce would calm her down—hopefully *not* by starting with, "You're not licensed."

"I had no clue that you were the brains of WD Consulting. Had I known, when I mentioned hiring these two to Cruz, I would've included you." Pryce threw the two men a sidelong glance. "Cruz had no objection. If he approves adding you to the team, then I'm fine with it. I don't want to do anything that will tee him off, so if he prefers to have you run the investigation, I'll give these two the boot."

Avery laughed. "If Cruzer decides to go with just me, I'll fire these two for you." Her cheeks pinkened. "I did send a few business cards over to him, advertising my new gig. He's scrambling because his regular guy told him to f-off. I asked what happened, but he had another call."

Harper and I were struggling not to laugh. Cruz was intimidating, and Avery was working on bestie status.

Seven turned Avery's chair to face him. "You and Cruz were chatting it up on the phone, and this is the first I'm hearing about it?"

"You know that he's one of my investment clients now." Avery made the zip lip motion.

"You two are engaged in a sit-down—his office, my guess—you're making suggestions for how to grow his already healthy net worth, and you slide in a pitch about your extended services?" Seven eyed Avery as though she were a perp.

"It didn't quite go like that." She let out a long sigh. "Getting him to focus on money is easy-peasy. Try to change to an unauthorized topic, and that's where you hit a stone wall. I had to come up with an alternate plan, and Pryce here was my entrée. Along with my newly updated resume, I sent over the reports I'd run on him. The credit report was for assurance that you could pay, since Cruz doesn't do freebies. All I wanted from him was a straight out yes or no on my new venture, since that's his general rep, and he weaseled."

"If you're doing reports, that's one thing — you'd be doing them anyway since you work for us. Unless you're branching out and not planning to tell us." Seven stared Avery down. To her credit, she didn't look away. "But if he's planning on sending you out on an investigation job that you're not trained for — which he may or may not know, depending on how you worded your *resume* — I'll kick his… If anything happened to you, I'd kill him. If he doesn't know that you lack training, I'll send him a text."

"I'm starting out small." Avery patted Seven's hand. "If I were to branch out, you'd be the first to know." None of us, including Pryce, believed her, because when Avery got an idea — one she thought was excellent — she went at it full force.

Harper eyed me holding Pryce's hand. "Are you sticking around or heading back to Palm Beach?"

"Pryce is staying right here," I answered for him. "I don't know where you're going with your questions, but before you start, why don't you tell him how you kidnapped Grey, held him hostage, and then the two of you hooked up?

And look at you two now. When you're done, Avery can regale Pryce with how she got charged with murder and hooked up with the detective here."

"You left out the part where Harper drugged me," Grey said with a smile.

"Please, you had it easy," Seven said, eyeroll in his tone. "All you had to do was lie there. I had to work to get my girl, make sure she understood she wasn't going anywhere without me."

Grey told his story, then Seven, which had Pryce laughing.

Chapter Five

The next morning, Pryce and I went to Cruz's office. I was pleased when he asked me to go along. One thing about the lawyer—he got to the point. His assistant brought Pryce a cup of coffee—I'd passed—and Cruz proceeded to shoot question after question at him, along with that dark-eyed stare of his. Pryce answered directly, not one waffly answer. Although Cruz took notes, he also recorded the conversation. What seemed like hours was actually just under one, and then he walked us out to his assistant's desk and said, "I'll be in touch."

The questioning was so intense that once behind the wheel of my SUV, I found the aspirin bottle at the bottom of my purse, took two, and held the bottle out to Pryce. He shook his head. "At least Cruz is direct and doesn't waste time. I suspect he was sizing you up with each answer you gave, and you passed." I handed the parking ticket to the attendant and zoomed out of the garage of Cruz's building. "I promised you lunch, and I'm taking you to one of my favorite places. Although it's a little out of the way, the drive along the water will make it worth the trip."

"I appreciate you coming with me." Pryce patted my hand. "It didn't take as long as I thought it would. A couple of times, I was tempted to check my watch but cringed at the thought of getting caught doing it."

"Awkward." I laughed. "It was interesting listening to Cruz lay out some of the evidence the prosecutor has against you." I maneuvered around a slow car and stayed in the lane closest to the water. "How did they build a murder case against you out of a recording someone supposedly made of you and Lili arguing on the beach and you threatening to kill her days before her murder?" I made a face.

"I'd like to hear the audio the prosecution shared with Cruz that's supposed to be Lili and me fighting, which he said was an overstatement since it was one-sided and over in under thirty seconds. It's good that Cruz wasn't impressed with the quality, but if the voices were clear, then the prosecutors would know it's not me." Pryce paused. "I recall passing a couple beachcombing, but they were never close enough to record anything."

"The recording doesn't worry me as much as the fact that they found her body in your old fishing boat in Coral Gables."

"One that I haven't owned in years." Pryce unleashed a disgruntled breath. "The killer must've thought I still owned the boat and put Lili inside to frame me. Apparently, the new owner didn't bother to update the registration. If he figures out that it's his boat being talked about in the news, you can bet we won't hear a word out of him."

"Or he sold it to someone else, and they didn't follow through."

"I'll have to see if I still have the bill of sale in my paperwork," Pryce mused. "When Cruz told us the prosecution theory is 'jilted groom gets even,' I wanted to laugh."

"You've got a number of witnesses on your side that can tell a different story, and with the exception of one argument, you two got along."

"What are the odds that Lili would be dumped on a boat I once owned? Then there's the rope they're still testing. Sorry about the gruesome details. Strangulation…" Pryce shook his head. "I want to go down there and check out every inch of the area." At my short shriek, he added, "I promised Cruz, and now you, that I'm not going to insinuate myself into any aspect of this case. Though it'll be hard."

"Back to the boat—it's highly probable that Avery can track the ownership, along with checking out the storage place in general. Someone has to know something; a few bucks might jog their memory."

"They do have security cameras," Pryce said. "Except that when the cops went to review them, they found they were broken."

"Another job for Avery—I'm betting she could easily hack into those cameras and see if there's any possibility of retrieving information. Worth a try."

"I'd have to get an okay from Seven before asking anything of Avery. I don't want to ask her to do anything that would land her in legal hot water."

"Also tell him that if Avery learns anything, all information will be turned over to him and Grey, and they can follow up. They know how to get answers out of people." My phone rang, and I glanced at the screen before answering. Thank goodness I had my earpiece in, since Harper didn't call often and my guess was she was probably up to something. "Pryce and I are on our way to lunch," I said upon answering.

"Avery and I were talking…"

I tried not to groan, but it slipped out.

"*Anyway*. You know my old author gig? I thought I could resurrect it to help Pryce. Keep an open mind until we talk about it."

In the hopes of uncovering information that would help in Grey's and Avery's murder cases, Harper had concocted a cover story about being an author researching her next project. Surprising how many people were willing to take her word in lieu of credentials and talk to her.

"Pryce and I will be back in a couple of hours, and we can talk then."

After a long pause, she said, "Okayyyyy."

"Don't do anything I wouldn't do."

Harper snorted and hung up.

"Is everything okay?" Pryce asked.

"I'm proposing a change of plans. We grab a quick taco and a margarita—and the place I'm thinking of also serves beer—then a rain check for something more upscale later." While Pryce tried to figure out what was going on, I pulled into the parking lot of a rundown blue-and-red building advertising "tacos" in bold letters on one side and "beer" on the other.

"What is this place? And how do you know about it?" He scrunched up his nose.

"Granted, it looks like a dump and possibly on the verge of being condemned, but until that happens, they serve the best tacos around. If you're squeamish, we don't have to sit inside." I pointed to a row of sloping umbrellas off to one side. Okay, so the trash cans lined up next to the fence were within arm's reach, but they didn't smell… or hadn't in the past. I parked and hopped out while Pryce gave the building a dubious stare. I knocked on the hood and crooked my finger.

He got out and started laughing. "I'm going to trust you on this one, but next time, I get to pick the place."

"Come on." I looped my arm through his. "Now's a good time to find out if I'm full of it on how good the food is. If we both get sick, I'll owe you an apology."

"You're not funny." He frowned.

"Not even a little." I led him through the small opening in the fence and claimed a table under a thatched umbrella. "I'll order for us," I said as the server approached. "Trust me." I laughed at his continued frown. "Two taco platters, everything on the side. I'll have a margarita, rocks, and he'll have a beer."

Pryce named a brand, and the served nodded and went inside.

"You got a call from Harper..." My eyebrows went up, as I hadn't told him who called. "Your phone was on the console—the screen's easy to read. Inside of a minute, plans changed. What are you up to? Let me rephrase that—what is she up to?"

Instead of answering, I tried for an innocent expression, which made him laugh. "Get used to asking that a lot when the three of us get together to work out an idea that one of us thinks is great."

Our drinks arrived. Pryce held out his bottle and I my glass. "To happy ever after." He blew me a kiss. "To us," he toasted.

"And to you being found not guilty, which I know will be forthcoming." I smiled at him over the rim of my glass.

It didn't take long for our food to arrive, the server setting down two large plates and silverware.

"If this taste as good as it smells, then this place isn't the irredeemable dump I pegged it for." Pryce took a cautious bite and nodded. "How did you find this place?"

"It's a local haunt. The residents around here keep it in business. You'd have to have lived here awhile to venture inside. In this case, looks are deceiving—you'd think it would attract trouble, but I'm not aware of any cop action."

"You were about to tell me about the sudden change of plans."

"I feel compelled to disclose up front that it wasn't my idea, but that doesn't mean it's a bad one." I ignored his groan. "And that it might test your resolve not to get involved in your own case."

"Grey warned me to be on my guard, that your friends would lure you into some scheme or another, although he wasn't specific about what. I'm thinking I should've asked for more details." By the way the food disappeared, I knew that Pryce thought I'd made a good choice.

"One thing about me—I don't generally jump in without looking at all sides. That said, I don't like being left behind. I'm thinking I should get you to agree to certain terms before I divulge anything, like keeping confidences."

"I'll have another beer," Pryce told the waiter,

who'd stopped back by our table. I waved off another drink. "Whatever you need me to say, or secrets you need me to keep, I'm in. Except if you're about to suggest something that would get you or one of your friends hurt or in trouble."

"To clear Grey, Harper came up with the idea of questioning those associated with the case, and in order to pull it off, she used the ruse that she was doing research for her next crime novel. I'll admit that she did let those she interviewed believe she was published, but surprisingly, no one thought to check on her. And so when Avery—" More groans from Pryce. "Open mind, please." I told him how Harper had resurrected her story for Avery's case and I went along as her sidekick. I did admit to being disappointed that no asked me any questions, which was probably good, since we hadn't come up with a good cover story for my involvement. "It's Harper's idea, or maybe Avery's, to resurrect her writer persona and go question anyone they can find associated with the case. I'd think Lili's mother would be at the top of the list. It's hard to stop those two when they get an idea, and from the excitement in Harper's voice, I'm thinking it's going to happen sooner rather than later, and I'd like to go along."

"You're my wife! What if you're recognized?"

"Since we don't want that to happen, I'll stay in the car. Harper and Avery have the coolest listening equipment, so I'll be able to hear every word. Which reminds me, I need to get my own."

"Do Grey and Seven know about this plan of theirs?"

"Calm down. Since Harper and Avery have trotted out this ruse a couple of times now, it wouldn't surprise me if they suspect, and if not, they will soon since they both keep close tabs on their girlfriends."

"We don't know anything about the supposed mother, and I wouldn't want anything to happen that you couldn't control."

"I get that, and I don't want anything to happen either." I absently patted his hand. "It's hard to deter either woman when they're ready to move. Especially Avery. Seven is the only one that can slow her down, and he does that by going along with her. Harper's slightly more cautious. From the little I got out of the phone conversation, and knowing them like I do, they've got something planned."

"None of this needs to involve you."

"I'm not being left out," I snapped. "I don't want to sit back and wait for a call to find out what they're up to."

Pryce sighed. "Did they say anything specific?" I shook my head. "So we don't know what they're up to, and it could possibly be nothing?" His brows went up.

I tried not to roll my eyes. He'd learn that when they got an idea, they acted on it.

"Before they do anything, they need to tell their respective significant others what they've concocted, or are about to do, or whatever stage their plans are in. I'm Grey's friend and wouldn't be much of one if I didn't give him a heads-up, which I'm not going to have to do because they're going to share their idea themselves."

"How about a compromise?" I waved off his response, certain it wouldn't be positive. "I agree with them telling the guys ahead of time, and I'm going to blame it all on you that they have to fess up."

"You thought I'd throw a fit, didn't you?"

Close. I tried not to laugh.

"Slight change of plans," Pryce continued. "I'll come along on anyone they decide to question, to keep you all out of trouble."

"That might work. But like me, you can't be seen anywhere near some of these people—I'm thinking especially Lili's mother and where she lived. Cruz would flip if he knew what we were talking about. You'll have to agree to stay in the car. Deal?"

The server came and cleared away the dishes. I handed her my credit card, and she headed back inside.

"Don't be surprised if, when you get home, you find those two have already snuck off and you have to hear the details after the fact," Pryce said.

"You're probably right, so..." I pulled my

phone out of my pocket and called Harper. "We're on our way back. Can you give me a slight hint about what you're up to?"

"Don't freak out. We're going to go talk to Lili's mother."

"I knew it." One of my thoughts anyway. "There's been a slight shift in plans." I told her that Pryce was coming with us and that they needed to update the guys.

"Grey already knows. He figured that I'd trot out my 'overused gig,' as he called it when he confronted me. I may sneak around a little tiny bit, but I don't lie."

I laughed. "And Avery?"

"If one knows, they both know," Harper said, as though that was obvious.

I laughed again.

"Pryce coming along will minimize the grouching." Harper had gotten over her irritation and now seemed to like the idea.

We hung up, and I repeated the conversation.

"You do know that if they didn't fess up and the guys found out that I knew, they'd take turns rearranging my face and I wouldn't blame them, right?" Pryce laughed humorlessly.

The server came back and handed me my card, and I signed the receipt. I stood and held out my hand. "Let's go home and find out what's going on."

He hooked his arm around my shoulders as we walked back to the car.

Chapter Six

I was as surprised as Pryce when we pulled into the garage and saw the doors of Harper's SUV standing open. Inching closer, we saw that she and Avery were sitting in the front. I backed into the space next to hers and rolled down the window. "I'm guessing you're ready to go?" I yelled across to her.

"We're wasting time," Harper yelled back.

Rolling up the window, I bit back my smile at Pryce's snort. "We could make a run for the elevator, but fair warning, they'll go without us, and then we won't get the whole story, just what they want to tell us."

"For some reason, I thought there would be a discussion of options before heading out," Pryce said with a shake of his head.

Knowing them as I did, I'd have been surprised if they hadn't had something up their sleeves all along and were never looking to have a *discussion*. "Most of the time, there's no slowing them down, so just hang on." I chuckled.

Harper honked, making a "hurry up" gesture out the door.

"Might as well." Pryce shrugged. "We both

want to know what Lili's mother has to say, and this seems to be the most expedient way to find out."

Pryce and I got out, walked over to Harper's SUV, and slid into the back seat.

"Took you long enough. What the heck were you two doing?" Avery asked, turning in her seat.

"We needed to finish making out." I grinned at Pryce, who side-hugged me.

"It's official, you two have decided to stay hitched?" Avery raised an eyebrow.

"We'll be sure to let you know when we've made our final decision."

At the same time, Pryce said, "Yes."

"If you ever need relationship advice…" Avery grinned. "Don't ask me. Seven thinks we're perfect; I think he's addled."

That elicited laughter from all of us.

"This is going to be fun," Avery said with assurance.

"You two might try acting a little more excited, since our little visit could yield useful information." Harper flew out of the garage to the highway, and from there, you'd have thought her tailpipe had caught fire from the way she maneuvered through the busy streets of Miami. Good thing she knew where she was going.

Pryce looked at me, his eyebrows in his hairline. I patted his knee and leaned over, whispering, "Harper's never gotten a ticket, or at least, not one she's admitted to." Okay, he didn't think that was funny.

"You two are going to be needing these." Avery shoved two earbuds between the seats.

I took them from her, rolling them across my palm and inspecting them closely. "Text me where you ordered these from. I'm going to need to start accumulating my own spy equipment." I handed one to Pryce.

"As long as you super swear that you'll take one of us with you on any snooping foray—" Harper flicked her finger between Avery and herself. "—you know you can borrow anything from me."

"I still want the ordering info." I grabbed my wallet out of my purse and handed Avery cash. At Pryce's questioning stare, I said, "Bribe money. More than once, we've found that it's easier to just offer people cash—a motivator to get to the good stuff."

"Harper, would you mind stopping at an ATM?" Pryce asked. "I'll get as much cash as you think you'll need, and Avery can give Rella her money back."

"It's not that big a deal." I shook my head.

"Yes, it is," he said adamantly.

Harper found a bank on the next corner and cruised into one of the drive-through lanes and up to the machine. Pryce rolled down the window, leaned out, and easily reached the display screen. It took a couple of minutes, and then we were back on the road, Pryce handing Avery the cash.

"Are you two going to share whatever plan you've cooked up?" I asked.

Avery turned in her seat. "As you've probably guessed, we're resurrecting the writer cover story. Once the mother finds out that we want to bring the murderer to justice, hopefully she'll give us insight into her daughter and, more importantly, who her friends were." Excitement bubbled in her topaz eyes.

"A trio of writers are going to converge on this woman's house, knock on her door hoping she's home—unless you were able to confirm that she would be—and start asking questions?" I asked.

"It's only going to be the two of us, since you're going to wait in the car," Avery said in an admonishing tone.

"That's what you think." I tried not to snap and barely succeeded. "I'll stand behind you two and won't say anything unless you need me to step in and be charming. He's my husband, after all." Pryce rubbed my lower back, which probably wasn't meant to signify his approval of my idea but more to slow down.

Once we cruised under the Interstate, the neighborhood took a decided turn for the worse. There was some cleanup and restoration going on, but it'd barely made a dent in the rundown area. Harper turned onto a side street with one apartment building after another. There was a smattering of cars parked along the long block, but not a person in sight. She pulled into a parking lot that bordered a rundown three-story building. A ten-foot wrought iron fence wrapped around the perimeter, and she parked on the far end. A young boy on a bicycle came out from behind the building, made several dizzying circles, then made his way out to the street.

"Do either of you know which apartment Doris Ford lives in?" I asked, scooting forward to look out the windshield.

"We know where we're going," Avery answered.

"I had a momentary lapse earlier—Pryce and I already agreed that it wouldn't be good if either of us were recognized snooping around. So I'm staying here and keeping Pryce company."

"Remember: no talking; it will only distract us." Harper turned and tapped her earpiece. "If you see us come running out of the building, be ready to make a speedy exit." She handed me her keys. "This is your first time as getaway driver, so don't get excited and ditch us." She ignored Pryce's glare. "You got your phone on you?" He nodded. She handed over hers. "Call yourself." She handed Avery a pen. "Put this in your pocket. It transmits to the phone and earpiece so you can see and hear everything going on. That way, there won't be any complaints about some bit of minutia failing to get mentioned."

Harper and Avery shoved the pens through

their buttonholes, and Harper tested to make sure that we were all hooked up.

"Listen up, you two." *For once* in Pryce's tone. "Be damn careful. If you suspect that anything is about to go awry, get back out here. Yell my name, and I'll come running."

Harper and Avery got out and went through the gate, which had been left cracked open, and up the walkway. Pryce and I moved to the front seat. He attached his phone to the holder that clipped to the visor, and watching it made it feel like we were standing in the middle of everything.

Avery took the lead and, after a glance around, pointed under the stairs. "Unit C is over here," she whispered. "Someone's home. The television's blaring." She knocked. "Home all right, since they just muted the TV."

Pryce's fingers tightened around mine as we heard the door squeak open, and a grey-haired woman poked her head out. Loud snoring could be heard coming from behind her. She gave Harper and Avery an assessing stare, not saying anything.

"Doris Ford?" Avery asked, and when the woman nodded, she stuck her hand out. "Sally Good, and this is Brenda Jones." She nodded toward Harper. "We hate to intrude at a time like this."

The woman stood mute as Harper stepped up. "We're reporters and wanted to do a story about your daughter, with an eye towards making sure that the killer ends up behind bars for the rest of his life. Where he belongs."

Pryce squeezed my hand and shot me a look that said exactly what I was thinking.

"Liliana was such a sweet girl," Doris cooed, her syrupy sweet tone in contrast to her hard and calculating eyes. "I'm certainly happy to offer any help. My name can't appear in the article, though—maybe after the trial. That awful man might come after me."

"We totally understand," Avery assured her. "We're happy to handle your involvement however you want, and that includes not mentioning you at all."

With one last look over her shoulder, Doris stepped out and closed the door. "I don't want to wake Hood up; he gets cranky when he hasn't had enough sleep." She stepped out into the sunlight and scanned the sidewalk, then motioned for them to follow her over to one of several empty planters, all filled with sand and cigarette butts. "We can sit here."

"Did Lili tell you why she cancelled the wedding?" Avery asked.

Caught off guard, the woman stared for so long, I didn't think she was going to answer. "It was a last-minute decision. I assume Lili was afraid of the man, and now look what's happened." She sniffed, swiping at the corners of her eyes.

I wondered if Harper and Avery noticed that she didn't seem to know Pryce's name.

"Is that what Lili told you?" Harper asked, a bite to her tone.

Doris looked at her vacantly.

"Except for her fiancé, was she having any problems with anyone else?" Avery asked, covering the awkward moment. "Do you have any reason to suspect that someone else might be the guilty party?"

Doris shook her head, once again slow to respond. "My Lili got along with everyone. A real people person." Her smile was calculating.

Avery asked more questions, and Doris took her sweet time answering them, always with a vague response. It was clear that the woman didn't know anything about her daughter's life, friends, or job, if Lili even had one.

"Am I getting paid?" Doris asked suddenly, licking her lips.

Avery pulled cash out of her pocket and handed it to the woman, and it disappeared down the front of her dress.

"My lawyer would have a cow if he knew I was even talking to you." Doris tapped her cheek, as though it'd just dawned on her. "We should definitely keep my involvement quiet. It's better that no one ever finds out how helpful I've been."

Pryce and I exchanged eyerolls.

"Lawyer?" Harper asked.

"Ferguson Waller. He says that fellow—Thornton, right?" Doris barely paused. "Anyway, the man's got big bucks, and it's only right that he takes care of me in my older years."

Pryce groaned.

"Waller? I've never heard of him, but I'm sure he'll do his best," Harper said, not sounding convinced.

"He assured me he's the best," Doris purred.

I'd bet that Waller was an ambulance chaser and the first one to track her down.

While Avery was thanking Doris for her time, Harper was already on the way back to the car, mumbling, "What a waste of time."

Pryce and I moved to the back seat.

"Even if this Waller person has filed the legal docs, it'll be impossible for him to get upstairs to serve you," I told Pryce. "No one can just stop by. Well, they can, but they have to be buzzed in from downstairs. And even if they manage to follow someone in, they can't get into the penthouse elevator without a key card. So if the buzzer goes off, be sure to check the security camera."

"You'd think that lawyer would have to wait for me to be found guilty before bringing a suit against me."

"Minor detail. You can be served anytime. How long the court would hold off on the trial is hard to know. My guess is that Doris and her lawyer would like an early settlement." I said with an eyeroll in my tone.

Harper and Avery slid into their seats.

"Got to give it to Doris—she knows how to give a non-answer," Harper grumbled. "I've run this con a time or two, and at least the people I interviewed previously actually knew the deceased enough to answer questions anyway, or give some nice version of 'none of your business.'" She started the car and cruised slowly to the exit. It was still quiet, except for a man walking a dog the size of a small horse.

"It didn't sound to me like she knew her daughter at all," I said.

Chapter Seven

Avery turned toward Pryce and me. "I'm assuming that you're flexible on time?"

Pryce grunted.

Taking that as a yes, she grabbed her phone and programmed in a new address.

I leaned forward but couldn't see the address, and looking at the map, it was hard to make out the destination.

"You might want to tell Rella and Pryce what you have planned," Harper told Avery.

"Since we're on the road, I was thinking why not check out Lili's apartment in Aventura," Avery said.

I looked at Pryce, who said, "She didn't live there—must've been a previous residence. The whole time Lili and I were together, she was living in a condo in Dania Beach."

Avery shook her head. "She moved about three months ago. And before that, she shared a house with a Wood Jordan. Contacted him, since he's the only one on the deed, and after some vague grumbling, the grouchy old man ended the call with 'Good riddance.'"

"I'm beginning to wonder if anything I knew about Lili was true," Pryce griped.

"How did you meet her?" I asked, leaning into him.

"It's been over a year now—a friend introduced us. We had a lot in common, never a disagreement about anything. Probably because she was too busy keeping her real self hidden. I have to wonder now." Pryce blew out a frustrated sigh.

"If Lili was smart at all and wanted to stay married to you, she would've had to continue keeping her secrets," Avery said. "Most won't fess up after the fact unless their hand's forced."

"Give Avery the name of the friend who introduced you, and she can run a check," Harper said. "Then she can forward the report to Grey and Seven, and they'll go talk to the man."

"Why not us?" Avery sniffed.

"For the same reason that we're not flying to the Bahamas to interrogate the hotel staff—the guys would flip out."

"Before we make the trek to Aventura, tell me what good it's going to do." Pryce glared at the back of Avery's head, since she'd turned back around. "You're gambling that she had a roommate, and that the person is home and willing to be interviewed."

"Maybe they have a key?" I smirked, knowing they didn't. What they did have was the next best thing.

"This is where I remind you that Harper and I have lockpicks and are proficient with them." Avery grinned.

I nudged the back of her seat. "I'm going to be needing one and a few lessons."

Pryce turned my face to his and shook his head. "I'm afraid those two will land you in jail."

"Hey," they yelped in unison.

"At least you know who to call if you're ever locked out of anything." I laughed.

Harper unleashed a loud groan. "According to my phone, there's an accident on the Interstate and traffic's backed up. I vote that we hold off on checking out Lili's condo until tomorrow. Early morning would be best—less likely to run into anyone wandering about, since we haven't had time to check out the neighborhood."

"Let's take a vote. We put this road trip off until tomorrow," Avery suggested. "Ayes?" All our hands shot up.

Harper found an opening and made a u-turn, then headed toward the beach.

My phone rang. I took it out of my pocket, glanced at the screen, and shook my head. *No way*. I hit the mute button and flipped it over. "That was about the tenth call from your Gram," I informed Harper. "As one of my best friends, you need to find out what she wants and deal with it for me. And whatever it is, tell her no thanks in a nice way."

Gram was Harper's grandmother, but she'd adopted us all.

Harper laughed. "You of all people should know that ignoring her won't make Gram go away. That plan fails every time. Gram's crafty, and when she does get ahold of you, and she will, she'll look all doe-eyed and sad and get exactly what she wants out of you."

"Agreed." Avery nodded. "You can say no until you're hoarse, and the woman will choose not to hear you."

I turned to Pryce. "You do know that this is most likely all your fault. Odds are that she heard I married a hottie and wants to meet you."

"How bad can it be that you're not taking the time to make one older woman happy by introducing her to his hotness?" Pryce grinned.

"Ha, ha." Avery shook her head. "It's never simple with Gram. She concocts some convoluted plan that sounds like endless fun and then springs it on you. I should know. The fun part... maybe for her." She winced. "If I were laying odds, I'd say it's either the wedding or Pryce's arrest—probably both. That's a twofer she can't pass up."

Pryce was still skeptical. He'd find out. We couldn't ignore her for long; she wouldn't allow it.

"Gram lives in a swanky retirement community on the beach, and she and her friends live for anything exciting," I said. "We'll definitely be expected to put in an appearance at some point. They'll want to check us out up close—primarily you, since they know me. I'm hoping my bestie can put her off as long as possible." I patted Harper's shoulder.

Her phone rang. Avery picked it up out of the cup holder, glanced at the screen, and held it up. "Speaking of…"

"If you answer, not a word that I'm sitting right here." *Please, I can't deal. Maybe next week or next month.*

"I'm not lying to Gram." Avery sent the call to voicemail. "She'd find out you were in the car and kill me for lying. And you know she'd find out."

"When you do talk to her, here's what you tell her—Pryce whisked me off for a honeymoon in Antarctica. He didn't mention a return date."

"Brrr." Pryce made a face. "This impromptu destination must've been your idea, as I would've come up with something warmer."

"Gram will see through that hokey excuse." Harper pulled around a car straddling two lanes. "Woman up and tell her in that CEO tone of yours, 'When my schedule opens up, you'll be my first call.'"

Sounded good, but saying it was another matter. I banged my head on Pryce's shoulder.

"Good luck with that," Avery whooshed. She would know, since she'd tried saying no before and knew firsthand it didn't work.

Pryce laughed.

"Go ahead and laugh," I said in a warning tone.

Chapter Eight

We'd gone home, by mutual agreement tabling all talk of Pryce's case, and parted ways in the hallway.

Turned out Pryce was good in the kitchen and whipped up dinner while I jokingly instructed him on what to do next, most of which he ignored, though he shot me a couple of smirks. We retired to the couch after cleaning up, and not one to watch a lot of television, I let him choose a movie—a comedy. The laughs were just what we needed.

An early riser, I headed to the kitchen the next morning to make coffee for the two of us. I perused the cupboards and decided a trip to the grocery store was necessary or we'd have to eat out, which was fun if you weren't doing it for every meal. Besides, I'd really enjoyed staying home last night.

Pryce slipped into the kitchen and onto a stool. His dark hair stuck up in a bad case of bed head, making him even sexier, if that was possible. Bruno trailed in after him and lay at his feet.

"We have a busy day," I said.

"Coffee first. I need it to think."

I filled a mug and set it in front of him, then got one for myself, sliding onto a stool across from him.

"How about we table the sleuthing for the day and go hang out in the sunshine — do something fun?" Pryce asked with a nod, liking his idea.

The front door hitting the wall had us both jumping, Pryce on his feet, ready to confront the intruder. More than one, I suspected.

"If there's a hole in the wall, be prepared to buy me a new wall," I yelled at the top of my lungs. Or a new door, except I liked the one I had.

"If you're nekked, you better cover up." Gram's voice cackled and echoed through the entry.

"What the devil?" Pryce strode from the kitchen, and I hurried after him, grabbing the back of his shirt and slowing him down just enough to stay at his side.

"Damn, you girls know how to pick the lookers," Gram squealed, giving Pryce a thorough head-to-toe perusal, then launched herself at him and wrapped her arms around his waist in a hug. Just when I thought she wasn't going to let go, she took a half-step back. "Jean Winters, but I insist you call me Gram," she said into his chest.

"Let the man breathe," I said in exasperation, shooting Harper, who was hot on her Gram's heels, a dirty look. *Make her behave.*

Harper held up her hands. "Gram used her key to get into my condo and, knowing where I keep my keys, snatched up yours, and…" She looked around. "Where did the bakery box go?"

"The entry table," Gram said, hooking her arm through Pryce's, who appeared somewhat amused after being thoroughly manhandled.

Harper backtracked and snatched up the box. "I'll just grab a bite of whatever you've brought and leave," she said, an *I told you this would happen* look on her face.

Not like this, I glared back, but she was already headed to the kitchen.

The door opened again, and Avery blew inside. At least the wall didn't take a hit this time. "Good thing I keep an eye on the video feed or I'd miss everything," she humphed.

This time, there was a knock at the door. "Did you want to get that?" Pryce asked Gram.

"You go right ahead." Gram patted his chest. "I'll divvy up the pie so we don't get squatty pieces."

Pryce moved around her as she hustled to the kitchen. He opened the door, and Grey and Seven strolled inside with smirks on their faces, not about to miss out on Gram's antics.

"It takes a while, but you get used to the 'what's yours is mine' attitude of these three." Grey clapped Pryce on the back. "Just know that it doesn't extend to *everything*." He and Seven laughed.

"When I heard Avery squeal and the door practically banged off the hinges, I suspected donuts might be involved in whatever's going on, as they're her downfall." Seven led the way to the kitchen.

Pryce was right behind him, and I couldn't hear what he said, but it resulted in more laughter from the guys. Avery had already disappeared into the kitchen.

Harper had gotten out the plates and lifted the lid on the box. "Key lime pie? For breakfast?" She eyed it suspiciously, taking it out and putting it on the counter.

Pryce made fresh coffee, and I got mugs.

"Couldn't come empty-handed." Gram gave us a toothy smile and took a seat at the island.

"To what do we owe this honor?" I asked Gram. I hadn't heard anyone ask that yet, even though I knew they all wanted to know. I turned and looked at the clock on the stove. "Seven am." *Who shows up that early? Gram. Making sure she has you cornered.*

"If you'd return a call once in a while—" Gram homed in on me. "—a woman of my advanced years wouldn't have to come up with an alternate plan, now would she?"

If that was meant to make me feel guilty... it worked, maybe a little. "There's been a lot going on." I returned her stare.

Gram turned her attention to Pryce. Giving him another appreciative once-over, she winked, and he smiled back at her. "It's a good thing I keep up on the news. Was anyone planning on calling me? Guess not." She directed the question around the table but answered it herself. "I'm probably the only one with questions, since the rest of you are up to date, but I say we hold off until we've all had a plate of sugar, which makes everyone more receptive, don't you think?"

Harper sliced the pie and served everyone. Pryce poured the coffee, and I got out juice and water and set everything in the middle of the island, all within arm's reach.

Gram took a few bites and sighed in pleasure. "The reason I'm here," she said over another forkful of whipped cream, "is I've got this amazing post-wedding party planned for the two of you. All you need to do is decide on the date. It surprised me to hear that you ran off and tied the knot. And with a drink or two involved? Harper yes, Avery maybe, but you…" She shook her head.

I hate you, I mouthed to Harper, who wasn't quite the drama queen her Gram was but close, so I knew where Gram had gotten her news.

"I told Gram that you'd known Pryce for ages and it was a love match." *So there* in Harper's tone. "I barely got the words out before she laughed. Her exact words were: 'What a load of…' Then she blurted out one outrageous guess after another. At that point, I thought, 'What the heck? Go with the truth.' Avery and I thought it was sexy and romantic, and so did Gram."

I leaned sideways and thumped my head against Pryce's shoulder. He looped his arm around me and held me upright. "It's nice that you want to throw Pryce and me a party, but—"

"You knock it off right there." Gram shot me a flinty stare. "No butts. You gypped us out of a wedding, which quite frankly surprises me, and if asked, I'm certain the girls would agree that a party's needed." Neither spoke up to refute her claim. "Who better to host said get-together than me? No one. I'll reserve the dining room at the pool; you know the layout and also know that there will be plenty of room for friends."

"As I was about to say, a wedding celebration is premature…" I turned to Pryce. *We haven't decided, have we?*

"We have decided," Pryce whispered in my ear, then turned my face to his and gave me a quick kiss.

"That's more like it." Gram cackled. "Premature? Whatever the heck that means. You're married. Make a damn effort. Besides, you two look cute together, and you'll make adorable babies." Gram checked us over and gave a nod of approval. "What do you think, young man?"

My cheeks burned.

"Ten children?" Pryce winked. I pinched his butt. "We'll agree to revisit the number."

"Listen up, all of you. I'm not getting any

younger, so I can compromise here. I'll scale down my party somewhat and host a big blowout later. You can't hardly object to a family dinner?"

If you'd known Gram for five minutes, you knew that once she got a *great idea*, she wasn't going to scale it back.

"As you know, Gramster—" Avery and Gram squared off. "—Rella's my best friend, equal to Harper, of course. I feel compelled to tell her that this is probably a trap. Not that she should say no, just beware."

I was just thinking… wasn't *family dinner* the same ruse Gram used on Avery? And then it turned out to be an untold number of people, all eager to stare at the 'murderer.'

Gram snorted and ignored her. "I need to know if this is a good time to catch the two of you at home," she told Pryce and me. "If we don't set a date now, I'll be back tomorrow… and of course, I'll bring breakfast. And every day after that until you decide. So you know, I'm not leaving with anything other than 'Love your idea, and we're in.' Along with a date, of course."

"I vote that nothing gets decided until tomorrow… or the next day." Harper licked her fork. "I'm requesting raspberry cheesecake next time."

"We'd love to come for a family dinner," Pryce told Gram with a wink. "You choose the date, and we'll be there."

I didn't bother to conceal my groan.

Harper looked down at her coffee and laughed.

Avery shook her head. "You were warned."

"Yeah, dude," Seven mumbled.

Grey nodded, fighting to control a laugh.

"Great news." Gram rubbed her hands together. "I've got the pool area reserved for a week from Saturday. I expect all of you to be there. No hokey excuses."

"Please promise that you won't go overboard?" I asked Gram, knowing the answer would be 'no chance' if she were truthful.

"Of course, dear." Gram fished out her keys, ready to get scheming.

"You know, Gram, since it's just family, we could have it here," I said.

"Nonsense." She jumped up and ran around the island, throwing her arms around Pryce, who was ready for her this time. "Welcome to the family."

"Remember: family only." Grey shook his finger at Gram, who beamed back at him.

We're screwed.

She kissed cheeks all around and flew to the door with a wave. It banged closed, signaling her departure.

"She's quite something." Pryce stood. "Coffee?" He grabbed the pot and filled the guys' mugs, the girls passing.

"You haven't seen anything yet." I blew out a breath.

"What Gram says and what she has planned are likely two different scenarios," Seven said. "Once you get over the shock that her initial description has nothing to do with actual events, you'll have a good time. She does know how to throw a party."

"Did Harper and Avery happen to mention what we did yesterday?" Pryce asked Grey and Seven.

"Harper's pretty good at sticking to her end of the agreement to keep me in the loop—most of the time anyway. For once, I'd actually heard about the planned ambushes ahead of time," Grey said.

"I'm betting it will come as a shock to all of you that I heard after the fact." Seven's stare bored into Avery.

"I appreciate the interest in my case, but I don't want them getting hurt," Pryce said. "They were lucky—the meeting with Lili's mother could've gone sideways, and I wasn't sure how I could've come to their aid if it did."

"In other words, butt out," Avery grouched.

"I agree with Pryce," I said. "It's not worth anyone getting maimed. So how about we agree to turn over all the visits to WD?" The suggestion was better coming from me than Pryce.

"The sleuthing trip we had scheduled for today needs to be put on hold," Pryce said, cutting the tension. "I've got a surprise for wifey." He grinned at me. "We might not get many opportunities to sneak away for a little fun, and now's the time to take advantage. We won't be back until late afternoon."

Harper and Avery, the romantics, loved that idea and smiled their approval at the two of us.

Chapter Nine

After everyone left, Pryce and I cleaned the kitchen and moved out to the couch on the balcony, where we stared out at the waves crashing on the shore, the water pulling back into the ocean.

"Were these surprise plans of yours a ruse to get off the subject of conducting our own investigations?" I gave Pryce a side glance and leaned my head against his shoulder. "I'm annoyed that we didn't check out the last address we had for Lili."

He chuckled. "Before Grey and Seven were out the door, I felt compelled to say that they have some real challenges on their hands, and I'd be shocked if they were told even half of what Harper and Avery get up to before they have to come clean. Good luck trying to keep up with those two."

"You're lucky you weren't overheard." I laughed. "Avery's a real wild spirit, but I believe that Seven wouldn't have her any other way. He enjoys chasing her down."

"There's a murderer out there, and if whoever it is gets wind of someone poking around in the case and feels threatened, who knows what they might do."

"Don't go anywhere." I jumped up, crossed to the entry closet, and came back with two shopping bags. I handed one to Pryce, then sat back down with the other one on my lap. "If we're disguised, there's no reason that we can't check out Lili's place, just the two of us."

Pryce pulled out a baseball hat and sunglasses.

"I got items similar to yours." I opened my bag. "We have to disguise your mug, since it's been all over the news. Although it's quieted down since there's been nothing to feed the interest. So it's likely we'll go unnoticed."

"Your *mug* has also made a newscast or two. The only reason the press isn't pounding down your door is because they haven't located your address, and even if they did, they couldn't get up here."

"The only way they'd get my home address is if someone who knows me gave it to them. Hopefully I don't know anyone who'd do that." More than ever, I was happy that no one could get up to this floor unless I authorized access. "I might've told you that I helped on Avery's case and know how to ask nosey questions." I ignored his smirk. "What do you really know about Lili's life? How does this Wood fellow fit in? There wasn't any reason for her to disclose everyone she dated, but lived with you'd have thought would get a mention. As for today's outing, I'm thinking we question the neighbors; nothing too intrusive."

"I admit to being very curious, since it appears that there's a lot about Lili I didn't know. As for Wood, what I got from the timeframe is that our relationships might have overlapped." Pryce leaned back with a big sigh. "Were there clues and I overlooked them?"

"Or she was just that good at deceiving people. You should give the guy that introduced the two of you a call and see if he's got any information on her life," I suggested.

"How about now?" Pryce pulled out his phone and scrolled across the screen. Before pushing "send," he flipped it toward me so I could see that it read "Michael Cord." I put my ear up next to his.

"Pryce here," he said when the man answered.

"Hey man, how're you doing? Heard what happened."

"Since you were the one to introduce me and Lili, I was hoping you could answer a few questions about her background. I've got a PI working the case, and we're trying to figure out who might've wanted her dead."

There was a long enough silence that Pryce checked the screen, and he and I exchanged a *What?* look.

Michael cleared his throat. "I'd forgotten all about that. But can't help you, since I can't remember the last time I talked to Lili. Just talking to you could get me dragged into the case, though chances are slim." He unleashed a nervous laugh. "And as I'm sure you've found out, it's bad for business. I'm certain you understand. If you're found not guilty, we can get together for lunch." He tossed out a rushed good-bye and hung up.

"If?" I practically yelled, then took a deep breath. "He's no friend."

"He can hold his breath waiting for that call. Thus far, I've only talked to my partners, and they've all been supportive and assured me that not one of our clients has brought up the subject of my arrest. As a venture capitalist, my clients need me more than the other way around. There's always someone needing money for their business. It's finding the ones we want to do business with that's the challenge. I imagine that there will be more of my so-called friends with the same attitude as Michael. The ones that count have already shown their support."

"If you run into Michael after your acquittal, make sure you give him the finger."

Pryce laughed and pulled me into a kiss.

I picked up the hat and put it on his head, along with the sunglasses. "Who are you again?"

He laughed again.

"Harper helped Grey with his case and Seven with Avery's, and I want to help you with yours. What could be better than the two of us working together?"

"Cruzer would have a stroke."

"Probably not, but I won't be the one to tell him."

"Here's the deal: drive-by only, and then we go to lunch." Pryce held out his hand, and we shook.

"I'm going to ask Avery if she can locate any friends of Lili's. Maybe one of them would be willing to divulge information. How we go about that... we've got time to come up with something."

"Forgot to tell you—Grey told me on the way out the door that Lili had a male roommate at the Aventura address that they're in the process of identifying, and they'll let me know what they find out."

"If that's true, it would be interesting to ask him a question or two," I said. Pryce's brows went up. "I'm not suggesting that we knock." I looked down at my t-shirt dress. "If lunch is on today's agenda, I'm going to need to change." I'd also stash a pair of tennis shoes in my bag, in case of... well, since we weren't looking for trouble, I hoped that I wouldn't need them. "It's still early enough to catch people before they leave for the day."

"Let's go."

I jumped up, ran to the bedroom, and slipped into a tropical sundress and a pair of sandals. I stood in front of the mirror and laughed at myself. Gone was the polished, professional attire and six-inch heels. I couldn't remember the last time I'd dressed so casually, and it felt good. I pulled my hair up into a ponytail and through the opening in the back of the baseball hat, donned my sunglasses and grabbed my purse, then went to meet Pryce, who'd changed into jeans and a t-shirt and stood waiting for me at the front door.

We rode down in the elevator and got into my SUV, and I slid behind the wheel—it'd turned out that he didn't care if he drove, and I liked to do it. Pryce programmed his phone and hung it from the mount that attached to the rearview mirror.

I grabbed him by the front of the shirt and pulled him into a quick kiss. "I'm thinking that we should keep this trip to ourselves. If we learn anything, you can share it with Grey and tell him not to out us. If he does, Harper and Avery will kill me, but before that happens, I'll blame you."

Pryce laughed. "You blame away; I think I can hold my own against those two."

On the way out of the garage, I noticed that Avery had already left but Harper's SUV was still in its space.

Chapter Ten

Traffic was light as I headed up the Causeway, the sun lighting up the blue waters that ran underneath and along both sides. It was a quick drive to the Interstate, where I turned north.

"Checked with Cruz, and there's no restrictions about where I'm able to go as long as I don't leave the state. I've talked to my partners every day since being released, but it's not the same as showing up at the office. If I need to put in an appearance, I'd like you to come with me so I can introduce you to my partners. They're eager to meet you."

"Then I'll take you to my office and do the same. It's just us girls, and they'll be excited to meet you."

The traffic snarled up in spots, but we made good time to Aventura, just north of Miami. We pulled into the parking lot of a newer two-story glass-and-chrome condo built around a grassy park-like area with easy access to all the front doors. I eased into a space in the front.

Pryce scooted up in his seat and stared out the window. "I know what you're thinking, but we already promised this would just be a drive-by. If someone sees past the glasses and hat and recognizes me, they'll call the cops — accused murderer in the neighborhood."

"We've been caught." I tugged on his sleeve, pointing out the side window. "I'd recognize that Porsche anywhere, even though I've only ridden in it a time or two." We watched as Avery, a militant look on her face, stomped over to the SUV and banged on the back passenger window. "I think she wants in."

"We're both going to be annoyed if she breaks the glass." Pryce hit the door locks.

Avery threw the door open, climbed in with a huff, and jerked it shut. "I can't believe you two were going to leave me out of this when I'm the one who's been tracking everything down."

We turned in our seats and watched as smoke blew out her ears.

"Your hair's going to catch fire if you don't calm down," I said. "If it makes you feel better, Pryce and I pre-agreed that this trip would only be a drive-by."

Avery snorted, making it sound like *sure.*

Pryce returned Avery's glare, not happy with her sudden appearance. "So, hotshot, what's your plan? If it smacks of illegal, I'm calling Seven." He held up his phone.

Avery huffed a long, aggrieved sigh, which must have hit Pryce in the face since he leaned back. "Who said anything about illegal? Okay, maybe a little bit. What good is a lockpick if you can't use it?"

"Yeah." I lightly punched Pryce, who wasn't amused.

"You looking to get your brains rearranged?" he demanded. "Which is what could happen if you walk in on someone."

"You've been watching too much television." Avery sniffed. "I'm the one with the most experience here."

Whatever. I looked Avery in the eyes and rolled mine. "I know you're eager to kickstart your new investigation career, but you need to slow down and think things through before acting."

"I've got a plan and a backup." *Bet you don't have either one* on her face. "Lili and I have been good friends for years, and hearing about her death…" She sniffed and wiped at the corner of one eye. "It's been so hard."

"You might want to dial it back a bit," I said.

"Anyway, I'll be knocking and offering my condolences. Then asking if I can get back a book I loaned Lili," Avery said, *meet with your approval?* in her tone.

"What happened to the writer gig?" Pryce demanded. "Don't you have to pick a story and stick with it? I'd think that way, you'd be certain of keeping your story straight."

"That's Harper's gig, and if she comes here, then she can roll it out. It doesn't hurt to have a backup."

"I can't believe you thought going to some stranger's door by yourself was a good idea. Especially when you have no clue what's on the other side," I said, attempting to tone down my irritation. "I can see on your face that you're hell-bent on going in, so good thing I'm ready with my disguise. I'll come with you." I got a glare from Pryce, but he didn't put up any objection.

"Give me your lockpick." He held out his hand. "Just in case. You've got breaking and entering on your mind. That's what the crime is called, in case you didn't know."

Avery ignored his request and instead pulled three earpieces out of her pocket and handed one to me and Pryce, hooking the other over her ear. "Since you probably weren't planning on getting out of the car and, my guess, didn't bring one with you — this way, you won't miss anything."

"Remind me to call in my order when I get home. I made a list of fun stuff, and they guarantee fast delivery." At Avery's raised eyebrows, I added, "I want my own spy equipment; what if you're not around, and I need something?"

Avery's only response was a shake of her head as she slid out of the car.

"You behave." I gave Pryce a quick kiss.

"That goes double. Seriously double. It's okay to cut and run."

I kissed him again, then got out and followed Avery down the walkway. She didn't break stride or pause as she headed to the last door on the end. It was an easy guess that she'd been here before.

Avery knocked politely. A minute later, the door opened, and a twenty-something stuck his head out, rubbing the sleep from his eyes. "Hey, ladies." He leered and opened the door wider, leaning against the frame. His baggy pajama bottoms hung low on his hips, showing off his bare chest and an intricate tattoo down one arm.

Avery stuck out her hand, and the two introduced themselves while I hung back. Turned out his name was Daniel. She offered her condolences, then launched into her speech about retrieving a book she'd loaned Lili.

Daniel asked the title, and she gave a response I knew she'd prepared in advance. He gave her a scrutinizing stare, barely giving me a look. "Honestly, we only have a few books lying around, and they're mine. But you're welcome to come in and have a look around."

That's a terrible idea, but before I could voice the thought, Avery shot inside. I was reluctant to follow, but did take a step forward and stood by the door, hand on the knob. The open-concept living room and kitchen were good-sized and the furnishings high-end, which fit with the upscale building.

Daniel's attention turned to me.

"Sorry about your girlfriend," I said and waited for him to correct me.

"We were best friends," Daniel said as he checked me out.

I nodded and pasted on a smile of commiseration.

"We haven't been introduced," he said and held out his hand.

I blinked in an attempt to cover the "deer in the headlights," managed to remember my pseudonym, and blurted out "Rachel," returning his handshake. Daniel's stare was so intense, I felt like he was memorizing everything about me and was thankful for the glasses and hat. I just hoped he hadn't seen through my attempt at a disguise.

"You remind me of someone. Were you a friend of Lili's?"

My stomach churned at the question. "I'm just tagging along."

"Nice place," Avery said, reappearing. "Love what you've done with the furniture. Also, great view." She pointed to the patio off the living room. "I hope you'll forgive me. I have to confess that I lied, and I hope you won't hold it against me."

I clenched my jaw to keep my mouth from falling open.

Daniel nodded, neither surprised nor upset by her admission.

"What the hell?" I heard Pryce say in my ear. I wanted to open the door and shoot outside, leaving Avery to deal with whatever was coming next.

"I'm a writer and researching Lili's murder in hopes of figuring out if they've got the right guy."

My eyes darted back and forth between Avery and Daniel.

"If Daniel looks ready to flip out, yell Avery's name," Pryce said, which I knew Avery heard as well.

"You're certainly ballsy." Daniel half-laughed. "To be blunt, I'm not interested in helping you or anyone get the Thornton fellow off. Far as I'm concerned, they arrested the right man." He turned to me. "How about we go to dinner and get to know each other better?"

"I'm married."

"I don't have a problem with that. What your husband doesn't know…" he winked.

Pryce growled.

I shrugged Daniel off with a nervous laugh.

Avery stepped between us. "Thank you for not going off over my misrepresentation." She pulled a business card out of her pocket and handed it to him. "If you change your mind…"

I skirted around him and out the door. There was something about that man—not bad-looking, but he gave off a creepy vibe, and that intense stare-down… I practically ran the short distance to the walkway, not slowing down until I reached it.

It took a few minutes for Avery to catch up to me. "You…" I started but stopped when she nudged my arm. I glanced back and saw that Daniel had followed us out. I waved, and there was that wink again. He followed us all the way to the sidewalk, but held back as we piled into the SUV. Then, he turned suddenly and headed back to his unit.

Pryce laughed. "Daniel got a little skittish and turned tail when I waved."

So that's why the hasty retreat.

"You want me to cruise the block a few times before dropping you off at your car?" I asked Avery as I backed out.

"The less Daniel knows about us the better." She turned in her seat. "Drop me off at the end of the driveway; he went back inside and can't see anything anyway."

"Why did you change stories?" I asked. "I'm surprised Daniel didn't flip, and instead took it in stride. I'm certain if it were me, I'd have had more of a 'What the heck?' reaction. But then, I wouldn't have let you in the house."

"Give a girl a break. I'm new at this." Avery snorted. "And Daniel was distracted since he was far more interested in you."

I pulled up to the curb and idled.

"If you're going to do any of your own snooping, you should think about a business card," Avery told me. "Learned that from Harper. I even threw up a website, and I'm thinking both will come in handy for any future gigs."

Pryce turned and stared at Avery. "My guess is that Seven doesn't know what you planned to do when you left the house this morning." Her blush was enough of an answer.

"Oh, Avery. He's going to kill you." I shook my head. "Don't worry, I'll come to your funeral and say something really nice: 'She was crazy but fun.' Something like that."

"That reminds me." Avery's voice was full of excitement.

Pryce and I glanced at each other, and we both grimaced.

He said dryly, "I'm certain you have a great idea about what to do next."

"You men and your sarcasm. But you don't like it when you're on the receiving end." Avery tapped me on the shoulder. "I've changed my mind—drop me off a block away, and I'll walk back."

Pryce gritted his teeth, clearly not liking that idea.

"You might as well get out here. We're not going anywhere until you're back in your car and on the road." I tapped impatiently on the steering wheel. "I sense you were about to say something else."

"I'm torn between calling and stopping by the funeral home where Lili's funeral was held—the latter might be better," Avery mused. "It makes it easier to bribe an underpaid employee for the guest list… if they keep such a thing. I'm about to find out."

"First off, how do you even know where the service took place? Second, don't you think that tactic is a bit vulgar?" I asked.

"I'm going to solve this case, and then you'll have to apologize and say that if it weren't for me… A party would be nice. Or donuts."

I hit the child safety locks a split second before Avery tried to open the door.

"Hey," she yelled, jerking on the handle.

I turned in my seat. "You're not getting out of this car until you tell us exactly where you're going."

"I'm going home." *Satisfied?* "I shot some video at Daniel's and want to watch it. You don't even have to ask—I'll forward you a copy. But only if you let me out of this car." She jerked on the handle again. "There were several framed pictures of Daniel and Lili in the bedroom. Happy now?"

"I would be if I thought you were really going home. You better be there when we get back from lunch or Seven will have to stand in line to off you." I shot her one last glare and unlocked the doors.

Avery didn't waste a second, jumping out, with a wave, and running for her car.

We waited until she was behind the wheel and followed her to the main highway, where she hit the gas, pulled a couple of maneuvers I didn't know she knew, and left us in her exhaust.

"I wouldn't be surprised if Seven drank, keeping up with her." Pryce pulled off the earpiece. "These are pretty cool. I agree with you that we need our own set. I almost had a heart attack when Avery changed the story. What was your reaction?"

"Tried to cover my surprise and hoped I didn't look stupid." I sighed; that was an intense moment. "Not sure I'm cut out for all this sleuthing and making up stuff last-second. I'm a terrible liar."

"Cruz did say that he didn't have to prove my innocence, just tear the evidence apart, rendering it useless and getting a not guilty. Don't forget: the superstar boasted he'd only lost one case." Pryce chuckled. "That tells us he knows what he's doing and we shouldn't do anything to screw up his defense."

"Unless someone else is brought to justice, you'll always be known as the guy who got off with the help of a high-priced attorney."

"Either way, people are going to talk until something more interesting happens or they get bored."

People could talk all they wanted as long as Pryce stayed out of jail. "I've already taken you to my favorite taco dive, so how about burgers? I know a place that's about a half-step up from the last one."

"You spoil me with these classy joints."
"Be warned: you have to share your fries."
Pryce laughed. "You're on."

Chapter Eleven

For the next several days, Pryce and I kept a low profile. When we weren't on the beach, we took our laptops out to the balcony and stayed on top of business remotely.

Gram called to let us know that she'd finalized all the plans for the "family party" and to mark our calendars for the upcoming weekend. She boasted of having planned every last detail, another way of guilting Pryce and I so we wouldn't back out. I might've tried if I could've come up with a good reason, but I couldn't think of anything... at least, not anything that wouldn't make me feel like a horrible human.

More than once, Pryce asked, "How bad could it be?"

"Just wait. Whatever you've conjured up about her being a sweet oldster without a solitary trick up her sleeve, all I can say is, I'll try not to tell you 'I told you so.' Since it's never satisfying."

With a laugh, he pulled me into a kiss.

Harper called with an invitation for dinner at her place and implied some kind of surprise but wouldn't give any details—just that Grey was barbecuing and the rest of us were to bring side dishes.

When Pryce and I finally ventured down the hallway, we were the last to arrive and everything had been set up out on the balcony. Knowing what we liked to drink, Harper handed me a dirty martini and Pryce a beer.

Grey'd had a ledge installed along the railing, and we all slid onto stools to enjoy our drinks, along with a view of the rippling waves below.

"I know you got a call from Gram, because we all did." Harper tipped her glass in my direction. "I'm thinking that we should carpool; I've got room for all of us in my car."

I leaned forward to make certain that she didn't miss the exaggerated eyeroll I gave her. "Thanks, but we'll be taking our own car," I said, not bothering to bite back the sarcasm. If the sandal were on her foot, she'd also want an easy getaway.

"I second that one. You've got to have your own ride," Avery said, slapping the table. "There's an exit at the back of the outdoor kitchen that will put you back on the road to Gram's house. From there, it's an easy jog to your car."

"Easy getaway after that," Seven said with a knowing nod.

"All right, you guys," Harper said. "There will be no sneaking anywhere."

Grey banged a utensil on the barbecue. "Grab a plate."

We moved to the dining table, and the conversation stayed drama-free while we ate, more than a few jokes going around that had us all laughing. Once the dishes were cleared away, we returned to our seats at the railing, each with a drink, and enjoyed the evening breeze.

"You might as well share your news," Harper said to Avery, then turned to us. "Believe me, I tried getting a preview out of her earlier, even played the friend card, but nope. Not even a hint."

"It's better to tell you all at the same time. That way, you can all get huffy together and get over it at the same time. The only one who got a preview was Seven, and that was to save my ears from a lecture."

Seven grasped Avery's hand and entwined their fingers. I knew as he had to that he didn't have her completely talked out of all the sneaking around, and since he'd signed up for the ride, he hadn't gone anywhere. The way the two looked at each other, it would take more than her going off on a wild hair to split them up.

"Went to a funeral, and it was a big, splashy affair, overflowing with guests." *Da-da-da* in her tone.

The reaction was unanimous — double-takes and disbelief.

Except for Grey, who slapped his hand on the

ledge. "If this has to do with Lili Ford, when are you going to leave the investigating to us?"

"Why don't you wait until you hear what Avery has to say, since getting one of our guys to go to a funeral wouldn't be a popular gig?" Seven said with a certain amount of amusement at his partner's annoyance.

"You knew all along, and not one word," Grey grouched.

"I promised Avery—"

"Whatever." Grey snapped.

Harper patted his arm.

"Okay, I've got an open mind," he muttered.

"Trust me when I say that one of your mountainous guys would've stood out and scared people," Avery said. "I went to the funeral home where they'd had the service for Lili just after the majority of the guests had arrived for another sendoff and crowded into the entry in groups. It was the job of a young guy whose name turned out to be Ben to get everyone to take a seat, but they weren't listening. I think he was new on the job, but I didn't ask." She wrinkled her nose. "I sidled up next to him and suggested that he yell, 'Sit down already,' which elicited a chuckle and then embarrassment."

"Didn't the parking lot full of cars deter you?" Harper asked.

"I figured that a busy time was the best, and it worked out." *So there* in Avery's tone.

"Did you by chance know the newly

CHAPTER

One

I STICK my finger into Bill's silicone butthole.

"What the hell?" Fabio exclaims in a horrified whisper. "That's poking. You have to be gentle. Loving."

Grunting in frustration, I jerk my hand away.

Bill's butthole makes a greedy slurping sound.

"See?" I say. "He misses my finger. It couldn't have been *that* bad."

"Look, Blue." Fabio narrows his amber eyes at me. "Do you want my help or not?"

"Fine." I lube up my finger and examine my target once more. Bill is a headless silicone torso with abs, a butt, and a hard dick—or is it a dildo?—sticking out, at least usually. Right now, the poor thing is smushed between Bill's stomach and my couch.

"How about you pretend it's your pussy?" Fabio's nose wrinkles in distaste. "I'm sure you don't jab *it* like an elevator button."

"I usually rub my clit when I masturbate," I mutter as I add more lube to my finger. "Or use a vibrator."

Fabio makes a gagging sound. "You're not paying me enough to listen to shit like that."

With a sigh, I circle my finger seductively around Bill's opening a few times, then slowly enter with just the tip of my index finger.

Fabio nods, so I edge the finger deeper, stopping when the first knuckle is in.

"Much better," he says. "Now aim between his belly button and cock."

I cringe. I hate the word "cock"—and everything else bird-related. Still, I do as he says.

Fabio dramatically shakes his head. "Don't bend the finger. This isn't a come-hither situation."

I pull my finger out and start all over.

My digit goes in rod straight this time.

"Huh," I say after I'm two knuckles deep. "There's something there. Feels like a walnut."

Fabio snorts. "That *is* a walnut, you dum-dum. I shoved it in there for educational purposes. The prostate—or P-spot—is around where you are now, but the real one feels softer and smoother. Now that you got it, massage gently."

As I pleasure Bill's walnut, Fabio shakes the dummy to simulate how a real man would be acting. Then he starts to voice Bill as well, using all of his porn-star acting ability.

"Bill" moans and groans until he has, as Fabio puts it, "a P-gasm to rule them all."

I remove my finger once again. I have mixed feelings about my accomplishment.

deceased? Or was it just some random—not sure what word to use—dead person?" I asked.

"Do you think not knowing anyone would stop Avery?" Harper laughed.

"If you keep interrupting me, I'm going to forget where I am in my story and have to start over." Avery shot us all a militant glare. "I managed to corner Ben again later. He wasn't too happy, since he was attempting to avoid me. Did you know that one of the entry-level jobs at a funeral home is door-greeter?"

"Do they advertise for that kind of job?" Harper asked.

"It's a family-run business, and Ben's related to one of the owners. I didn't ask too many personal questions, since he was already nervous and I didn't want him bolting, as the only other options were a couple of older men who didn't look the least bit approachable."

"How did you bring up Lili's funeral without raising red flags?" Grey asked.

"Once everyone was seated and the doors were closed, I was able to get a minute with Ben. Knowing that I had to make it quick, I just asked him straight out: 'Do you have any way of knowing who showed up at the Ford funeral?' He looked faint, but then I flashed some cash."

I shook my head. *How did she not get thrown out?*

"I went into my book spiel and assured him that I wouldn't tell anyone and assumed he wouldn't be talking either, so it was our secret. Turns out they make notes of everyone in attendance and keep it in a file. I handed him my business card and wrapped his fingers around more cash. Told him it was just for trying and not to do anything stupid. Feeling like I'd pressed my luck as far as I could, I told him, 'Call or text,' and bolted out of there." Avery downed her vodka on the rocks and handed the empty glass to Seven. "Refill, please."

"You're not getting sauced until you finish your story." He took her glass and set it next to his.

"Two days later, he texted a picture of one page with three signatures on it. I had to wonder if that was a complete list of the guests that showed up. To those who are about to ask, no, I didn't go back, call, or bother him again in any way."

"Tell everyone what you found out about the names." Seven smirked.

"You're fired," Grey snapped at him.

"You can't do that," Avery snapped back. "You're partners."

Seven leaned back, enjoying their sparring.

After glaring at Grey a moment, Avery went on. "Daniel was one of the names, and the other two were older women that live in the same building. No relationship that I could find, so I'm assuming neighbors or friends."

"Can't decide if it was gutsy or just plain nuts

that you went to the funeral home," I said, shuddering at the thought.

Avery looked at me like she'd heard that too many times and was tired of it.

"It's hard to believe that you went straight back out the front door after going to all the trouble of getting in," Harper said.

"Well... Ben got a text and had to run off. After he left, I headed to the door. Taking a turn down a long hall, I saw an exit sign and headed that way. There were several doors along the hall, but all were locked, except for the last one. In that room, some dude was propped up in a coffin. It was creepy, but at least he was staring at the wall and not me."

I grimaced and buried my face against Pryce's shoulder. The last thing I wanted was that image stuck in my head.

"I'll make a note that you're available for funeral crashing," Grey said.

The conversation finally moved on to less morbid topics.

I squeezed Pryce's thigh and, when he turned, telegraphed, *Let's go*. Then stood in case he hadn't gotten the message, but he was right beside me. "We'll see you tomorrow."

"You should reconsider carpooling and, while you're doing that, remember that Gram doesn't tolerate lateness." Harper tapped her watch.

"Please... I know I've reminded you several times, but just one more time. Tell Gram 'low-key.' In fact, call her right now and remind her that there were witnesses to her swearing she wouldn't overdo it. If that doesn't work, tell her you overheard Pryce say that if there were any unexpected surprises, he'd divorce me."

Pryce laughed.

"Good one." Avery gave me a thumbs up.

"No worries. Gram and I talked, and we're in complete agreement," Harper assured me.

Chapter Twelve

It was Saturday, the day of Gram's party. I found a dress bag at the back of the closet, something I'd purchased and never worn, and shimmied into the peach spaghetti-strap dress, noting that it was flattering in all the right places. Dressed in black slacks and a crisp white dress shirt, Pryce stepped up behind me, his reflection joining mine in the mirror as he zipped up the dress. Then I scooped my hair off my neck and whipped it into a messy bun.

He turned me around and kissed me. "After a quick chat with Seven, I've formulated our exit plan."

I threw my arms around him and gave him a hard hug.

He linked his arm in mine, and we walked out the front door, surprised to find our friends waiting for us at the elevator.

I wondered how long they'd been there but didn't ask.

Harper tapped her watch. "I was about to suggest that Grey pound on your door."

Grey gave her a side-eye but didn't appear annoyed.

"I would've volunteered." Avery raised her hand.

Seven pulled her to his side.

Pryce checked his watch and looped his arm around me. "And look, now we've wasted another minute."

Harper ignored him. The rest laughed.

The six of us got in the waiting elevator and rode down together. "There's no reason we can't ride to Gram's together," Harper said.

"Just ignore her," I said, loud enough for all to hear. Once the door opened, I grabbed Pryce's hand, beelined straight for my SUV, and got behind the wheel. When we both had the doors closed, I hit the locks.

I was certain that if Harper were behind the wheel, she'd follow me north to Ft. Lauderdale; with Grey driving, we followed him. Traffic was at a minimum today, which made the drive short. We exited and headed towards the water. Morningside by the Beach was an upscale retirement community on the A1A across the highway from the beach and boasted an unobstructed view of the water.

Grey turned in, and because we had stickers on our windows, the guard raised the security arm as soon as he saw us and waved as we cruised past. We followed the circular drive to Gram's unit, her red collector '57 Thunderbird in the driveway.

Pryce whistled. "You think Gram will take us for a ride?"

"Probably not, since I've never seen anyone in it except for her, but you're welcome to ask." I smirked.

"Remind me which of your friends can hotwire a car?" Pryce eyed it as we slipped into a visitor space.

"Gram would kill Harper, and it wouldn't matter that she's her only granddaughter."

Pryce laughed.

I leaned over the console and brushed his lips with a kiss. "There'll be some new faces, as Gram will have invited a few of her neighbors. I've met most of Gram's friends, and they're a fun bunch, which is true of most living here at Morningside."

"Ready?" Pryce asked, and I nodded.

We got out and joined the rest of our friends in the driveway. At the same time, the front door flew open, and Gram ran out and hugged us all. She was dressed in a cream-colored A-line chiffon dress better suited to something more formal than a get-together by the pool.

"Come in." Gram motioned to us, leading the way inside. The door of the two-bedroom unit opened into a living room/dining room space with the kitchen off to one side. It had its own patio with a small grassy area in the back.

Taking a cautious look around, I was surprised to see no other guests.

"Looks like Gram kept her word," Pryce whispered.

One hoped, but I couldn't help thinking about the party she'd thrown Avery, which started out the same way. I stepped forward and enveloped her in another hug. "Thank you for keeping this get-together low-key."

Gram blushed, but I didn't know if it was from what I said or the fact that Pryce winked at her.

"Call out your drink orders," she said, giving Grey a slight push over to the bar built into one wall of the dining room. "We need to toast the new couple." She hustled into the kitchen, yelling, "I'm getting the ice."

I claimed the loveseat and tugged on Pryce's hand so he sat next to me. "I'll take a martini." I waved at Grey. "Make it really dirty."

Gram came rushing back out of the kitchen and served the drinks as fast as Grey got them made.

Pryce tipped his glass against mine with a wink.

Once everyone had a drink, Gram moved to the center of the room, glass raised. "To our newest couple. I predict a long and happy union."

Everyone tilted their glasses. The guys had some kind of non-verbal code going, which included trading smirks.

Gram clapped her hands. "As you know, I've

arranged for us to have lunch out by the pool. It's time for us to make our way down there. But first…" She walked over to a side table, picked up a white box tied with a matching satin ribbon, and handed it to me.

I hesitated, staring at it like it was about to explode. Pryce's nudge had me reaching for it, certain my frozen smile looked stupid. I refrained from shaking it, setting it in my lap and taking off the ribbon. I parted the tissue and lifted out a white tulle veil with lace appliqué flowers around the edge, holding it up for all to see. "It's beautiful." *But why?*

Gram took it out of my hands, set it on my head, and arranged it around my shoulders. "So perfect for the day." She ran and grabbed another box, this one larger. She opened it and pulled out three cream straw hats shaped like dinner plates, with silk flowers and feathers in the middle. She handed one each to Harper and Avery, then pinned one on her own head. "Don't you just love these?"

"I guess this means I get to kiss the bride again." Pryce leaned in and brushed my lips with his.

"Aww." Gram almost swooned. She grabbed my hand and led me over to the mirror, where she fussed with the veil, which hung past my shoulders, looking far dressier than my dress. Gram hung her head over my shoulder and smiled. I turned and hugged her.

It amused me to see that Harper and Avery were having a hard time getting their plates to sit on their heads. Catching a glimpse of their struggles in the mirror, Gram let out a snort and stomped over to them, taking something out of her pocket and anchoring the hats in place.

Avery snorted. "We probably could've figured it out if you'd given us all the pieces."

"Deprive me of my fun? I don't think so." Gram motioned for all of us to stand, throwing her hands in the air. "Get your rumps up and let's get this party started." When she got to the door, she came to an abrupt stop and turned. "This is follow-the-leader, and the leader would be me." *Got it?* in her tone. She led the way to the driveway and stopped again. There, she lined us up—Harper and Grey behind her, then Avery and Seven, and Pryce and I taking up the rear.

"She's up to something," Pryce whispered.

I struggled not to roll my eyes.

Gram led us over to the pool, where four older women waited at the gate. When they caught sight of us, they snapped to attention. One had a boombox tucked under one arm; the other three had baskets in their hands.

We were within a foot of them when *Here Comes the Bride* started blaring through the speakers.

Pryce pulled me into a hug and laughed in my ear. "It's not a death march—smile." He demonstrated.

I took a deep breath, the warm, salty air filling my lungs, wishing I was over on the white sand. There was barely a cloud in the baby blue sky. Noting the flower-laced arbor, a lone man standing underneath facing us, I turned to Pryce and smiled. "I think we're getting married again."

"Will you marry me? Again," Pryce asked with a teasing wink.

"Yes." We both smiled, and then our eyes met and we laughed.

The women with the baskets stepped toward the arbor and threw what appeared to be birdseed to each side of the aisle. Gram motioned the rest of us forward.

On our way up the aisle, I notice at least a hundred people—a quick count failed to provide an exact number—their chairs turned, drinks in hand and excitement on their faces. A number of them, I recognized—everyone from my office had turned out. They all waved, wide grins on their faces. I bet they were looking forward to having a good story to tell about this. Pryce and I came to a stop in front of an older gentleman, a double for Jimmy Buffet in shorts, a tropical shirt, and a worn baseball cap. "Dearly beloved—"

"Let's skip to the good part," Pryce whispered to the preacher or actor or…?

"Do you…"

We faced one another and exchanged vows,

my voice soft, Pryce's full of conviction.

"You may kiss the bride."

Pryce pushed my veil behind my shoulders, wrapped his arms around me, and bent me backwards, giving me a kiss that had the guests catcalling and whistling. We turned and waved, receiving a raucous round of applause.

We started back down the aisle to the encouraging shouts of our guests. Gram met us, wiping her eyes, and steered us to the head table — the largest of the lot and the only one with place cards. The pool area was dotted with a number of smaller ones, all under thatched umbrellas.

"You have a rather large family; hope I can keep the names straight." Something or someone caught Pryce's eye, and he covered his surprise and waved, a big grin on his face. "Gram invited my partners. How did she…?"

"If only she'd taped the conversation… My guess is she ordered them not to ruin the day by being no-shows." I chuckled. "Everyone from my office is here. And there's still plenty of people that I have no clue about. A double martini, please," I told the waiter who swung by our table before we could even get seated.

"Maybe she called one of those rent-a-guest places." Pryce laughed in my ear.

"Probably posted a flyer in the common area: 'More fun than you can handle' and, of course, free food and drink." Pryce would learn soon enough what a schemer Gram was. "Hang onto your shorts, babes... or in your case, pants." I eyed him with a brow wiggle. "No telling where this is headed, and I'd be surprised if Gram doesn't have another trick or two up her sleeve." He laughed even harder.

With the help of the birdseed ladies, Gram directed everyone to a table. It appeared there was a strict seating arrangement. Pryce and I took our seats at the head table, along with the rest of our friends. Gram, who stood at the opposite end, banged on the table with a spoon. "Everyone," she shouted in a gravelly voice. "Now, listen up. I'd like to introduce you to Pryce and Rella Thornton. Aren't they the cutest?"

The guests clapped and hooted, including a few more that were seated around the pool.

Pryce stood and, raising his voice, said, "This is where I concur — yes, we are." Which garnered more whistles. He pulled me up and hugged me hard to his side, then waved, and I followed suit. His laugh was contagious and calmed me down as I laughed along with him. Nervousness gone, I dropped my corporate face and managed to relax.

"Kiss... KISS!" someone shouted, and the rest joined in, clapping.

Pryce spun me around and swooped me back into a kiss that met with appreciative whistles.

Before we could sit back down, Gram

maneuvered between us, grabbing our hands, and led us around to the different tables, introducing us to those we didn't know, all residents of Morningside. Gram's introductions were unorthodox, just like the woman herself.

"Rella's a do-gooder—always raising money for one cause or another," Gram introduced me to several people at one table. "These folks are willing to part with a buck or two for a good cause." I smiled politely. Pryce chuckled.

All kinds of comments floated our way.

"Little quick, wasn't it?"

"Last time I saw you, you hadn't had a date in ages."

I scolded my cheeks for turning red, for all the good that did.

"You're a murderer," someone yelled. I struggled not to flinch. Pryce tightened his hold on my hand. To his credit, he maintained an easygoing smile.

"Not guilty," another woman shouted, leering.

"I read where you shot her point-blank. You get blood on your clothes?" This one from a man.

Pryce waved to get everyone's attention. "I have an announcement," he said, loud enough to make sure everyone in the pool area could hear. "So that there's no misunderstanding, I didn't kill anyone."

There were more than a few disappointed groans.

We finally ended up at the tables where our

coworkers were seated. I introduced Pryce, and he did the same for me. The two tables decided to merge so they could trade stories.

"If you can't think of anything nice, make something up," Pryce told his friends, who all laughed.

"We're going to have everyone over for dinner at some point," I promised.

They all looked pleased at that idea.

"Well, this is *another* murder party you've overhyped," an older man complained to Gram.

"Don't pay attention to one word this man says." Gram stepped in front of the man in question, leaning down to kiss his cheek. "This is Harper's father—Edgar Finn. I raised her, which is why she turned out so well."

"I'll admit that I was late to the parenting party, but I had a hand in raising the amazing woman she turned out to be." Edgar's eyes sought out Harper, and he winked at her. "You'll see me around the office from time to time, as I own the building. Treat Rella right, or I'll make you disappear."

Gram moved us along to the next table.

I was in awe of Pryce, who charmed men and women alike. A number of them asked if he was sure he hadn't killed anyone, but his smile never slipped.

"So much for meeting a real felon," one grumbled.

Just then, I saw that food was about to be

served and tugged on Pryce's arm, heading back to the main table.

Our friends looked up with identical smirks when we arrived, and Avery assured me, "They're an easy audience. You just need to know that they like anything outrageous. I don't even think they care if it's true or not." She joined the laughter at her comment.

"You two worked the guests like pros," Harper lauded Pryce and me. "It was easy to see that you won them over one by one. You'll be the talk around here for a long while, and that will cement Gram's 'favorite' status."

"While everyone's enjoying the amazing food, I say we sneak out of here," I said.

Pryce pulled out my chair. "I can't be seen as an unfriendly murderer."

Chapter Thirteen

Later that week, Pryce and I took our mugs and laptops and spent the morning on the balcony. We divided up the table, spread out, and clicked away madly while drinking coffee. Pryce had thought to bring the coffee pot outside, so we didn't have to go far for a refill.

He had a conference call with his partners, and once everyone was online, I leaned sideways and waved. I ignored my own work and listened in on his meeting, trying not to be obvious. I was impressed that despite the amount of business that was discussed, there were plenty of light moments. It was clear that the men, and two women, got along and respected each other.

My email pinged with a file that needed my attention. There was a fundraiser coming up, and several issues needed to be dealt with before the big night. Then my phone rang with a call from the office, and I got up and took it inside. Thankfully, all the fires were easy to put out, and it didn't take long before I was back outside, disappointed to see that Pryce had hung up.

"Next time, I can add you to the meeting if you'd like, and you can give us feedback," he said with a raised eyebrow.

Caught me. "Sorry I couldn't stay until the end. I would've taken my call out here, but I didn't think either of us would be able to hear anything."

"I've never spent this much time out of the office before, and I'm not missing it. I'm surprised that I've managed to stay on top of everything, and I like it this way."

"Same here." I nodded, also surprised that I didn't miss my focus always being on work.

"I can't believe that we haven't been invaded yet." Pryce glanced over his shoulder at the front door.

"I warned Harper and Avery that if they come bursting through the door, it better be a verified emergency or something dreadful that I left unspecified would happen. And that going forward, we knock first no matter what, and they agreed."

"Uh-huh." Pryce laughed, not convinced. "What are your plans for the rest of the day?"

"I've been thinking…"

He groaned, shaking his head. "Is this where I remind you of our promise to each other?"

I made a face. "Keep an open mind."

"I'm listening. As long as we're in agreement before moving forward on whatever you've cooked up."

"What if we made a trip to Dania Beach and talked to Wood Jordan? According to Avery, he wasn't happy about how the relationship ended with Lili. Be interesting to know what happened. I've been thinking about it, and it wouldn't be any more nervy than what we've already done and might give us more insight into who Lili was."

"Now *you're* going to be a writer?" Pryce asked, his tone conveying that he thought the idea overused.

"How about the truth? Lay it out there and see if Mr. Jordan will talk to me. He might be sympathetic if he feels like he was the victim in the relationship."

"You're going to knock on the man's door and tell him you're the wife of the man accused of offing his ex, and would he mind answering a few questions?" I nodded. "And by chance, were you the one that strangled her?"

"I've been thinking..." I tapped my temple. Pryce wasn't amused. "We beef up your disguise, and I'll pass you off as my bodyguard."

"Why not let WD send someone to question the man?"

"I haven't heard Mr. Jordan's name mentioned by either Grey or Seven. In fact, they never discuss the case at all, so it's hard to know what they're doing and not doing."

"They keep me updated, but Jordan's name hasn't been mentioned. Thus far, they haven't uncovered any smoking guns, but not for lack of trying."

"There's also the fun factor—the two of us working together to prove your innocence. Personally, I don't want to look back on this time and remember only sitting back and watching."

Pryce looked around. "Where's my disguise?"

"Don't go anywhere." I jumped up and ran into the living room, opening a drawer in the buffet and grabbing a shopping bag, then going back outside and handing it to Pryce.

He pulled out a fake mustache and a pair of thick-lensed glasses.

I laughed as he put on the glasses and held the mustache up to his lip. "Don't forget your baseball hat."

Pryce took a sniff of the mustache and wrinkled his nose. "I vote that we take some time to think about this idea."

"Except that I was thinking today would be a good day to sneak away, since I happen to know that our friends are otherwise occupied and if they notice we've left, they'll think we went out for lunch. If they don't know about our outing, then we don't have to share unless we want too."

"You do know that when Avery finds out, she's not going to be happy with you, don't you?" He stood and held out his hand, and we went inside.

* * *

My preference would've been to drive along the

coast, but that would've taken hours, depending on the traffic. Instead, I hopped on a toll road that took us north to Dania Beach. There were plenty of cars headed in the same direction, and everyone moved along at a fairly fast clip.

We exited and headed toward the Atlantic Ocean, then turned into an upscale residential neighborhood a couple of miles before we ended up at the water. There were newer two-story houses mixed in with single-story ones original to the neighborhood. All the houses had large green yards, flower beds, and palm trees, all in top shape.

Mr. Jordan's home, a cream-colored single-story Spanish-style house, had an inviting brick driveway that could hold several cars but was currently empty. I cruised slowly to the corner to check out the rest of the quiet neighborhood, then turned around and came back, parking in front of the house.

"Are you sure about this?" Pryce asked.

"The alternative is for you to put on an earpiece and stay in the car." I'd placed an order with the spy gadget website and requested overnight delivery, but we hadn't had a chance to test anything out. I reached for my purse.

He batted my hand down. "There's not a chance in hell that I'm sitting out here. Besides, this mustache has irritated my lip and the corners of my mouth non-stop; I should get something in return for the annoyance."

"Once we're back home, I'll kiss it and make it better." I opened the door, and he grabbed my arm.

"If anything goes sideways, don't hesitate, just run. We'll figure out what to tell the police later."

We got out and started up the driveway. "Since you're my bodyguard, you need to walk behind me." I smiled at his grunt. "I did some research—"

"I bet you did." Pryce slowed to half a step behind me. "I hope Jordan's not home," he grumped.

I smoothed down my sundress, and before ringing the doorbell, I turned. "One more trick—don't make eye contact."

"That won't be hard, since I can't see anything through these glasses."

A sixty-something opened the door, television blaring behind him. His cranky demeanor let us know his day hadn't gotten off to a good start. "Whatever you're selling, not interested." He started to shut the door.

I held my hand out. "Mr. Jordan, this is a bit unorthodox." I ignored the quiet snort coming from behind me. "If you'll give me two minutes, then you can kick the door shut."

The man stared for a long, uncomfortable moment. "You've got one minute." He moved to block the doorway.

"I'm the wife of the man accused of murdering Lili Ford." Jordan's brows shot up, but he remained silent. "I'm hoping that you might know of someone who had a motive."

"You mean someone other than me?"

"I never thought—" Jordan waved me off. "I was thinking you knew her well enough to tell me something about who she knew and who might have wanted to hurt her."

"Cops showed up here and might've arrested me, since I couldn't think of a nice thing to say about her, except that, lucky me, I had an alibi. It was my regular poker night." Other than a cursory glance, he barely looked at Pryce.

"I believe in my husband's innocence. Though this might not have been my best idea, I want to do something to help him. I'm just trying to find someone who knew Lili well enough to tell me about her and what she was like."

"That Thornton man is well rid of her," Jordan said in disgust. Noting my look of surprise, he added, "Oh yeah, I've followed all the coverage. I don't have an ounce of sympathy for Lili, but I wouldn't have killed her."

"Can I ask what happened between the two of you? I won't be the least bit offended if you tell me to mind my own business."

Jordan half-chuckled. "Lili Ford was a con artist, and there's no other, nicer, way to put it. I thought I was the one pursuing her, but looking back, I came to realize it was the other way around. Her plan was to fleece me, I guess thinking I was so besotted that when a few items went missing, I wouldn't notice. What she didn't know was that I have security cameras in this house, and when I noticed an expensive watch had disappeared, I sat down to watch the footage. To my shock, it showed her ransacking my house, pocketing several items. After she'd gone through the place once, and apparently frustrated she wasn't finding enough of value, she made a call in the middle of her thieving and asked questions about how to get the safe open."

"And did she?"

"Hell no," Jordan said. "I confronted her with the footage, and she didn't show the slightest bit of contrition. I'd already packed her things and told her I never wanted to see her again. That's when she boasted that she forged a couple of my checks and said if I tried to come after her, she'd make me the laughingstock of the neighborhood. She specifically mentioned the golf club where I'm a member."

At a loss for words, I said, "I'm sorry."

He shook his head. "I barely restrained myself from drop-kicking her out the door. I checked my accounts and had to give her credit for an excellent forgery. I closed everything and opened new ones. I thought about pursuing legal options but knew she'd make good on her threats and considered the stolen money a payoff. She was so slick that I knew I wasn't her first patsy."

"How long were the two of you together?" I asked. When he gave the dates, I felt Pryce stiffen behind me — they'd been with her at the same time. "My husband feels like he didn't even know her at all."

"That's one thing we have in common." Jordan was now scrutinizing Pryce more closely. "Interesting you should show up. Some woman called last night — said she was writing a book or some such — and I hung up on her. Didn't quite believe what she was selling."

"I know what you mean. I talked to that same woman. Like you, I didn't believe her." Good thing Avery wasn't here.

"I never met any of Lili's friends, though she met a few of mine. Told me she was a loner after the death of her family — car accident, if that was true."

"Thank you for giving me way more than my allotted time." I smiled.

"I'd tell you to be careful of Lili, but she's dead. Good luck to your husband." Jordan took one last long look at Pryce and went back inside.

I walked down the driveway and back to the car, Pryce behind me. I slid behind the wheel, and when Pryce was in and the doors were closed, I said, "Wow. I have a stomachache." I pulled away from the curb.

"Jordan warmed up to you, even though I'd already bet against it and expected him to kick us off the doorstep. Caught him staring my way a time or two like I was one of those infamous Florida roaches."

"It's up to you whether you want to tell Grey and Seven."

"They need to know, but I'll do it privately."

Chapter Fourteen

A couple of days later, I took my coffee out to the balcony and took a seat at the railing overlooking Biscayne Bay. The sun had risen a few hours ago, and its rays reflected off the water below. I preferred to start my day with a morning drink and the sight of the waves rolling onto the shore. This was my favorite time of the day. This right here. Clearing my mind. I was waiting for Pryce to finish his conference call and join me. I'd already had a short call with my office and tied up loose ends.

Pryce came up behind me and wrapped his arms around me. "Since it's a perfect day for a walk, let's go before it gets scorching hot." He grabbed my hand, and the two of us raced out the door and took the shortcut to the beach.

The baby-blue sky was filled with white, fluffy clouds, and the view only got better as we trekked closer to Miami Beach, the whitecap waves of the Atlantic crashing onto the white sand.

"My sixth sense tells me that Avery is up to something." I kicked water on Pryce's legs.

He ran after me, picking me up and twirling

me around before he set me back down as a smaller wave lapped the shore. "That woman is always up to something."

"The three of us went on a donut run early this morning; she got a phone call and, after looking at the screen, left the table. When she got back, she was about to burst from excitement, but didn't say a word. When I tried to question her, she jumped up, saying she needed to get something sugary to take home to Seven."

"What did Harper say?"

"She blew it off, saying, 'She probably discovered a new investment. You know how excited she gets over that.' I felt like I'd been told 'none of your biz' by both of them. Trust me when I tell you that I know I'm right and I'm going to dig around until I uncover what Avery's up to. And if it turns out to be about your case, which I suspect it is, then we're going to have a talk. I wouldn't be so suspicious except she hasn't mentioned your case in days."

"However you plan to get her to talk, I hope it's legal." Pryce stepped in front of me and stared down.

I shook my finger at him, which he nibbled on. "I won't be put off." I pulled my phone out of my pocket and sent a text. "Just told her we're coming by the office for a tour. That sounds plausible, and you'll get to see where everyone works." I sent a second text to Harper.

"Avery's not going to be happy if she smells a

setup, although she won't be able to resist finding out what you're up to."

"Do you think if the high heel was on her foot, she'd let me off? Except she doesn't wear them, claiming they make her nose bleed. Though I haven't witnessed that. I did ask her to take a picture and got a snort for an answer."

"This should be interesting, barging in on Grey and Seven at the office. Better than one of their homes and catching them naked."

"Now that would be an eyeful." I winked at him, then grabbed his hand and tugged him toward home. He didn't make it easy, laughing at my attempts. I finally got behind and gave him a push.

He turned on me, tossed me over his shoulder, and ran up the sand.

* * *

On the way to the office, I decided to pull a Gram and take a key lime pie. All that sugar would put everyone in a good mood.

After picking up the pie, I avoided the traffic, eventually turning onto the one-way street where the square four-story white stucco office building sat, just short of a freeway underpass. I slowed turning into the parking lot—not another car in sight, but I knew that everyone who worked in the building parked in the underground garage.

Pryce craned his neck, checking out the

exterior. "There's a brewery here?" He inclined his head up at the billboard that sat on top of the building.

"Harper's father apparently wasn't interested in chasing advertising, and the billboard hasn't been changed since he bought it; not sure if that place is still open." I pulled into a parking space to one side of the entrance that led to the offices on the upper floors. "Since Avery appointed herself building manager, it surprises me that she hasn't rented out the ad space. She doesn't like anything that's not profitable."

"So what businesses are here?" Pryce asked, noting the lack of signage.

"First floor is a cleaning business, and their entrance is around the front." Where they had a sign that could be seen from the street. "Avery took over the second floor for her business—AE Financial. WD Consulting is on the third floor. And the fourth floor is storage," I said, getting out and opening the back for the pie box. "The neighborhood looks iffy, but it's pretty quiet,"

"Who are we going to get to let us in?" Pryce's finger hovered over the call box, which had numbers by the buttons but no names.

I held up three fingers. Seconds later, the door clicked open.

When the elevator got to the third floor, Seven already had the door open and motioned us inside.

Grey, who was on the phone, waved.

I handed Seven the pie. "We'll need plates and silverware."

Hs sniffed the box. "Bribery?"

I ignored his question. "Be sure you save a piece for Dixon." Avery had recently brought the man on as a partner. He was another one who lived to decipher math problems that didn't appear to have an answer. I sat down and sent Avery an *I'm here* text. Then added, *Third floor.* "Okay, we should be invaded any minute." The guys laughed.

The door flew open, and Avery blew in, Harper behind her. "I thought you were coming to my office," Avery said, throwing herself in a chair.

"There's pie." I pointed to the strip kitchen. "And a piece is being saved for Dixon."

"It works for me if any of you want to bring pie by every day," Grey joked after hanging up.

Harper crossed the room, cut the pie into slices, and passed them around. "You know, burgers would've gone good with this." She licked her lips.

"Next time." I was tempted to roll my eyes.

Seven pulled over enough chairs that we were able to all sit around Grey's desk.

"Yell out what you want to drink," Harper said. We were split evenly between water and coffee, the guys going for the latter.

Grey eyed me suspiciously. "You've never just stopped by before."

"What has Avery done now?" Seven directed the question to her.

"I object." She slapped her hand on the desk.

"I will apologize, maybe, if you can look us all in the eye and tell us with a straight face that you're not up to anything," I said. "Don't rehash things we already know about—we want to know about any surprises you're about to pop out of your pocket."

Seven stared at her over a spoonful of pie. "I'd be interested to hear your answer."

"Me too." Grey eyed his bite of pie, but ate it anyway. "Let's hope this isn't another last-to-know story."

"I'm feeling ganged up on." Avery made a sad face.

"I'm in support of holding you hostage until you spill." Seven's lips quirked.

"You've been caught, so you might as well come clean," Harper said. "Besides, where's the Avery that's always outing herself, proud of her latest scheme?"

"None of you are funny." Avery downed the rest of her water, pitching the bottle in the trash. "I want it on the record that I discussed my new idea with Seven and Grey and got approval. Ahead of time." At my and Pryce's groan, she added, "Somewhat, anyway. Where was I? Oh yes. I had this idea—"

"Why don't you hop to the good part, before we all forget what we're talking about?" Harper made a circling motion.

"It so happens that I was able to track down the two women that signed the guest book at Lili's funeral—Millie Edwin and Olive Frank. I spoke with Millie, and they've both agreed to be interviewed for my article." Avery sounded proud of her score.

"Article? What happened to your book?" I asked.

"You know it could be either," she insisted. "I've been testing to see which one gets a better response. Or I can shorten it to just writer, and that way, I can't be caught in a lie."

Pryce groaned. "You're certain that Seven and Grey sanctioned this latest scheme of yours?"

"Scheme is harsh!" Avery glared at him. Seven hooked his arm around her and gave her a reassuring pat.

"It was kind of shocking when Avery came to us with her idea, since it was the first time we were hearing about something before it happened." Grey maintained a straight face, though the sides of his lips quirked. "Seven and I agreed that the women might feel more comfortable talking to another woman, and if anyone could get them to talk, it would be Avery. Actually, any of you could probably get them talking."

"When I contacted Millie, she was reluctant to speak at first," Avery continued. "To get her to agree to a sit-down, I offered to bring something from the French Bakery, and she oohed over that and asked if she could invite Olive. That made it easy for me, since she was going to be my next call."

"Neither woman had any stipulations?" Grey asked.

"I had to promise that no one would find out about their involvement. They're worried, since they live in the same building as Daniel and don't want him finding out. They told me that it was a gossipy building, all the neighbors up in everyone else's business, and if anyone found out, everyone would know in an hour."

"I'm happy that we don't have that problem in our building," I said, and Harper nodded.

"You were supposed to get back to us with the day and time of this meeting," Seven reminded Avery.

"Today," she squeaked. "Come on, you guys, you were on board with the idea from the beginning."

Seven turned her chin to face him. "It only stays a good idea if you give the right answer to my next question. Are you planning on going by yourself?"

"They're two older women; how much trouble could they possibly be?" Avery asked, the face of innocence.

"I'm surprised that your boyfriends don't drink," Pryce quipped.

I pursed my lips, attempting to hide a laugh.

"Hey, why am I finding out about the call along with the rest of you? Shouldn't I be one of the first to know?" Harper asked.

"You already agreed that talking to them was a good idea," Avery reminded her. "My plan is to go by myself—that way, I can come and go without being noticed. If I drag those two along like last time—" She pointed to me and Pryce. "—someone's going to see through their lame disguises, and I won't get a chance to ask the women any questions."

Harper clapped me on the back with a laugh. "That's easily fixable—a new disguise."

"I don't want to crush your enthusiasm," Seven said. "But if these women didn't actually know Lili... well, gossip doesn't tend to be helpful, as it's not reliable."

"The more people we can talk to, the better our chances of uncovering someone with a better motive than being dumped at the altar." Avery raised an eyebrow at Pryce. "I'm hoping for more information about Lili's life than what we know now. Considering the double life she was leading, it's highly possible that it will lead to other suspects. If I talk to more people, we can fit the pieces together and get a better idea of who this woman was and all the things she was capable of. We can't ask Pryce, as he doesn't seem to know... unless he's holding out."

Pryce ignored that, instead asking, "If Daniel sees you? His next question is going to be, 'What the heck are you doing back?'"

"I'm opting for a disguise, even though I probably don't need one. For this trip, I've got a blond wig and sequin glasses that cover most of my face." Avery drew two circles on her face to indicate how big they were.

"I thought that was for…" Seven grinned.

Avery shot him a squint-eye, and he winked.

"This is easily solved." I waved my hand. "I'll tag along, and you can introduce me as your beleaguered assistant. Two women in a nice neighborhood won't attract attention."

"Count me in." Harper raised her hand.

"Three of you showing up?" Pryce shook his head. "How are you going to explain that?"

"Just me," Avery said adamantly.

"Should something go sideways, are you prepared to defend yourself?" Seven asked.

"No backtracking—you already said it was a good idea." Avery air-boxed. "I was in a fight once." All eyes shot to her with disbelief. "More like hair-pulling and shoving, but still. Fairly certain, if it comes to it, I can take two women who sounded Gram's age."

I flinched at that image. "I say that you do whatever it takes to avoid a fight, and that includes running."

"There's only one thing to do…" Pryce turned to Grey. "You're fired. I appreciate everything you've done. Time to let Cruz's man do all the uncovering of information."

Avery shrieked and jumped up, kicking back her chair. "I didn't mean for you to jump ship." She waved to Harper, *Help me out here* on her face. "You can't do that. Besides, Cruz recently signed on with WD."

"Calm down." I waved my arms around like I was half-nuts. "No one's going anywhere until we figure this out and everyone's happy."

"When does that ever work?" Harper grumbled.

After much back and forth between the guys—going over every little bit of minutia while the girls and I made faces at one another until we laughed, which garnered stares that we ignored—Pryce growled, "Attention, ladies. By a unanimous vote, it's been decided that I'll go along with whoever's going. Any dissenters can stay home."

Avery glared so hard, it was surprising he didn't combust.

"You were a big hit with the ladies at Morningside," Harper reminded him. "If there's an awkward moment, pour on the charm… or take your shirt off."

Pryce flexed his muscles.

"Unlike our brawler, Avery, I've never hit anyone or pulled their hair, but if someone were to get handsy…" I threw a punch in the air.

Pryce grinned.

Chapter Fifteen

Everything was cleaned up and we were ready to leave when Avery's phone rang. She looked at the screen with a raised brow, then stepped over to Seven's desk and turned her back to answer. It was a short call, during which she said very little.

After hanging up, she turned to faced us. "That was Millie. Something's come up, and she'll call me to reschedule. I know a brush-off when I hear one and will be surprised if she contacts me again." She was brimming with irritation. "I'm going back to my office." She stormed out with barely a good-bye.

"I've got this," Seven said, hot on her heels.

"Seven's got a meeting with a new client in an hour, and it wouldn't surprise me if he takes Avery along with him," Grey told us. "She's new to this game and is going to find out that more people than she'd like will flake on her."

Harper moved around Grey's desk and sat in front of him.

"Rella and I are leaving." Pryce grabbed my hand. "I'll see you guys in the gym in the morning."

Grey nodded, but his attention was occupied with Harper.

A cell phone on Seven's desk rang. Recognizing it as Avery's, after a moment's hesitation, I withdrew my hand from Pryce's and grabbed it. No one paid any attention, thinking it was mine.

"Hello," I said tentatively, after glancing at the unidentified number. I'd lost my mind, answering someone else's phone. I wanted to say that Avery would do the same, but would she? I made my way out of the office and into the hallway, Pryce following and closing the door behind us. How to explain to him?

"This is Olive, Millie's friend, and we got to talking... Sorry to be so indecisive, but we got cold feet because we don't know you. We'd like to be of help. Only it can't be today because something really did come up."

"I completely understand," I said sympathetically, thinking she had a valid point.

"We were both excited to be interviewed for your story, so I pushed to reschedule. That's if you want to."

The elevator doors opened, but I waved at them, not wanting to step inside and lose the signal. "How about if we meet at a neutral location? I promised dessert from the French Bakery—what if we were to meet there for lunch, my treat?" I asked.

Pryce's eyebrows had gone up, and he hung

on every word. At least he wasn't scowling or making grouchy noises.

"We'd both love that, having heard so many great comments about the place. You know it's rather expensive," she whispered conspiratorially.

"No worries about that. I can charge it off as a business expense."

"Well now, love that. If you're sure?"

"When's a good day for you?" I asked.

"Hold on a second." Olive turned away from the phone but didn't lower her voice. "Millie, tomorrow good for you? We'll be meeting at the French place. How fun is that?" She bubbled with excitement, then made a few unidentifiable sounds and came back on the line. "Eleven-thirty so we don't have to wait in line?"

"Perfect. So you know you have the right person, I'm a blonde and will have on a hot-pink dress."

"You're a dear for being so nice about the change of plans."

"Very happy that you called back. I look forward to meeting you and Millie." We hung up. I took another look at the phone and then pocketed it. Now what to tell Pryce?

He'd been holding the elevator door open, and I followed him inside. "I can't wait to hear what that was all about."

Another idea struck me, and I took the phone back out and scrolled through the images. Sure enough, there were pictures of two older women that had been sent to the phone earlier today. I forwarded them to my phone and pocketed it again. "I have a dilemma."

Pryce hit the button for the bottom floor. When the doors opened, we got off and went outside to the car.

I put the key in the ignition and turned to Pryce, confessing what I'd done. "The right thing to do is go up to the second floor and return her phone, but then Avery will know what I did. But if I don't, how do I explain keeping her phone?"

Pryce held out his hand. "I happen to know a trick or two." I handed it over. "I'll delete the call, so no explanation necessary. For now. If it's your plan not to tell her at all, my guess is that at some point, Avery's going to figure it out, and then she'll be tempted to commit bodily harm." He scrolled across the screen and, a few taps later, handed it back.

"I'm going to run this upstairs." I hopped out of the car and bypassed the elevator. I knocked at Avery's office and, without waiting, threw open the door. Avery was sitting on Seven's lap. "I'm certain that you're looking for this." I handed her the phone.

"Thank you. So frustrated about earlier," she said. "We'll talk later."

Seven winked at me.

"Later. Pryce is waiting." I hustled back out and down the stairs. Getting in the car, I said,

"This is your case—you should decide how we move forward."

"Let's go home and out on the balcony, have a cold drink, and discuss options."

Chapter Sixteen

The next morning, while the guys worked out in the gym several floors down, I called an emergency meeting with Harper and Avery. I told them we'd be walking on the beach, thinking it would be an easy sell, since it was one of our favorite places, but both had a host of questions before they agreed, all of which I ignored. "If you're a no-show, then don't complain about being the last to know or not knowing at all." I ended the calls with a polite good-bye.

It didn't surprise me when they both showed up.

"This better be good." Harper eyed me suspiciously as we walked down to the water.

I ran ahead and turned to face my friends, bringing them to a halt. "I've done something totally shifty and need to confess." My eyes moved back and forth between the two women, then focused on Avery. "You know that I picked up your phone in the WD offices yesterday, but what you don't know is that I took a call and let the caller believe that I was you."

Harper smirked.

Avery's mouth dropped open. "That's something I'd do. That said, I don't like that it happened to me. Who the heck was it?"

I repeated the call close to word-for-word, as I'd gone over everything multiple times when I couldn't sleep.

"Today?" Avery made a face. I nodded. "I can't go." She turned and kicked at the water. "Seven thinks I've been way too pushy, which I kind of agree about. Under threat of being cuffed and dragged, I agreed to go on a client call with him today. He promised that it wouldn't be as boring as the one yesterday."

"Don't be mad," I implored. "I don't know what came over me — I guess I got caught up, and after getting a taste of excitement the other day, I wanted more, especially knowing it might help Pryce."

"You did something else that we don't know about?" Harper practically yelled.

"Lower your voice," I admonished.

"There's no one out here but us." *Duh* in Avery's tone. "Spill."

"I think Pryce is telling the guys; if not, then I'm thinking keep it a secret. Try anyway." Both had *hurry it up* looks on their face. "Pryce and I went to Wood Jordan's house. Pryce posed as my bodyguard, but I think the man saw through the disguise and just didn't call him out on it."

Avery stamped her foot in the sand. "Mr. Jordan totally blew me off when I called."

"You trot out the writer gig?" Harper asked, amused that her recycled idea was getting used once again.

"I came up with a new cover — the truth. For the most part. I did leave out a few pertinent details, such as my name, but Mr. Jordan can look it up if he wants."

"The truth?" they both practically shrieked.

"I introduced myself as the accused murderer's wife."

"Let me guess, Jordan invited you in for coffee and you just… what?" Avery demanded.

"We stayed on the front porch, and good thing because Pryce, would never have let me go inside." I went on to share everything Jordan said. Both were shaking their heads by the time I was done.

"Bet Pryce is happy that Lili ditched him at the altar," Avery said. "Wonder why she was so money-grubby? Possibly because she didn't have any of her own, but still… I haven't been able to find any record of a job."

"A short marriage could be one way to deal with money issues," Harper said. "That plan might work once, but after that, I could see multiple marriages becoming a problem." She made a face.

"The more Pryce learns about the woman, the more wigged out he gets," I said. "Nothing he knew about her was true. To think he almost married a woman he didn't really know."

"Then turned around and married a complete stranger," Harper pointed out. "So not the best choice under normal circumstances, and so totally out of character for you."

"I can't explain what the heck came over me. But despite all the drama, I haven't regretted a day."

"You two look really happy together." Avery beamed, and Harper nodded.

"Back to why I brought the two of you out here…"

"I have a great idea for your meeting today," Harper said, motioning for us to continue our walk. "No, I'm not suggesting that I go along. That would irk Grey, and sometimes it's hard to tease him out of a mood." She made a face. "They're older women and reluctant to meet a stranger—good for them. I say you invite the ultimate icebreaker: Gram. If anyone can get someone to spill everything they know, it's her."

"It's so last-minute, I'd be embarrassed to ask."

"Nonsense." Harper pulled her phone out of her pocket and made a call. "Gram, you up for a free lunch?" She laughed. "No, not me. It's Rella, and be sure you give her a hard time before enthusiastically agreeing." She handed me the phone.

I dug my toes into the sand and told her what was going on, then had to hold the phone away from my ear while she squealed her excitement.

"You know how to make this girl's day." More squealing when she found out the restaurant. "One of my favorites." A big sigh came through the phone. "Don't you worry about me. I'll do you proud."

"I think I just bumped you off the top of her favorites list," I said after we hung up. "Am I forgiven?" I asked Avery.

"As long as you bring me dessert—the tiramisu."

"Done." I hugged her, and we continued our walk.

Chapter Seventeen

Pryce and I met up after his workout and each confided to the other that we'd updated our friends with the latest happenings, then went to change for lunch.

"How did you leave everything with Avery?" Pryce asked as we rode down in the elevator.

I drove out of the garage and cut over to the highway that ran along the water. I itched to wander down to the cool blue water of the Atlantic and spend the day with Pryce, my toes wiggling in the sand.

"Didn't get away without having to super swear to update Avery and Harper in great detail. The only reason Avery isn't in the backseat or riding our bumper is that Seven has her under his eagle eye today. Even so, it wouldn't surprise me if she showed up at the restaurant."

"She'll have to save whatever sneak-away trick she's come up with for another day. Seven's got a surprise that he guarantees will please her. I tried to dig for a few details, since I did wonder if it had to do with my case, but my questions were rebuffed with a laugh that made me want to punch him. He was enjoying annoying me so much that I wasn't going to give him the satisfaction."

"Is this a version of guy humor—get on each other's nerves?" I asked.

"Pretty much." Pryce laughed reluctantly. "I should've brought this up sooner... Don't want to be a party pooper, but I'm not certain that getting together with these women is a good idea. We don't know them or what they're capable of. It's not too late to turn around."

"It is too late. Nobody bails last-minute, especially when they're probably waiting on me. Besides, we're only blocks away, and I've got this covered. Nothing's going to go awry."

"Uh-huh." Pryce didn't sound convinced. "When they find out there's no story, book, whatever and it's a con for information, then what?"

"That's when you ramp up the charm and sweep them off their feet. Figuratively speaking."

"If they start screaming murderer, I'll beat it out the back exit, and you can pick me up around the corner."

"And if the cops swarm the place?" I laughed.

Pryce grimaced. "Go on the run and hope I make it back to your place, which would be quite a trek on foot."

"If it comes to a manhunt, I suggest that you cut over to the beach and follow it back."

"So glad you think this is funny."

I easily found parking on the street on the same block as the restaurant and turned slightly when he opened the door. "I thought you were sitting in the car?"

"I didn't wear this itchy mustache to sit in the car. Or these coke-bottle glasses I just purchased." He pulled them out of his pocket and put them on. "These are ugly enough, but I can see through them, unlike those other things."

I handed Pryce his baseball hat so he could model his tweaked appearance. Looking at him, I tried not to laugh and decided not to point out that the round frames made him look cross-eyed. I wondered if that feature cost extra. My guess was that Avery had recommended the store where he purchased them, since she'd had an eyeglasses fetish pre-Seven.

"Do you know which story Avery used when she called the woman?" Pryce asked.

"She's switched between stories on almost every contact she's made, and it's highly possible that she doesn't remember, since I got a vague response when I asked. The truth worked with Mr. Jordan, so I'm going to try it again." I followed Pryce's finger as he pointed out the windshield. Gram was coming briskly down the sidewalk. I rolled down the window and waved wildly.

"Did you know Jean was going to be here?" Pryce asked, suspicion in his tone.

Oops. I'd forgotten to fill him in on this part of

today's outing. "If you want your ears boxed, keep using her first name. If you don't believe me, go ahead and ignore my warning." I shot him a shifty smile and got out. "She's everyone's Gram, so just go with it." I closed the door on his response.

Gram met me at the bumper, and I threw my arms around her and smothered her in a hug.

Pryce came up behind us and enveloped us in a three-way hug. "Since I'm the last to know, why doesn't one of you catch me up on what's going on?"

"Harper thought Gram's presence would make the other women more comfortable and get them to open up," I said as we headed to the restaurant.

"This is going to be fun." Gram rubbed her hands together. "Talked to Harper again, and she cautioned me not to come on like a steamroller. So happy to be part of the ruse."

"No… it's not going to be like that," Pryce cautioned.

"Don't be a spoilsport before we've even got our feet wet." Gram squinted at him. "Besides, I was under the impression that you were cooling your own feet in the car." She pointed behind him, in case he'd forgotten where we parked.

I bit my lip.

"Who's going to admire my disguise if I'm sitting in the car?" Pryce straightened his glasses.

Gram stepped in front of him and leaned in,

flicking at the mustache. "Hate to break it to you, but it looks like a strip of dirt that has stray hairs hanging off the sides. And the glasses... *butt ugly*." She whispered the last part. "If you were wanting to disguise your hotness, you scored. Now you're... maybe not woof material but..." She barked.

I swallowed a laugh. "Gram, you need to behave." I gave her a squint-eye. She grinned. "We're sticking to the story I ran by you on the phone, and I'll remind you that you agreed. I'm not good at keeping track of lies, hence the truth, or close anyway."

"Yeah, yeah. I got it," Gram said impatiently. "Just know that if you need to turn south, I'll follow."

Why do I think Gram already has a plan of her own that she isn't about to share until she unveils it? And that'll be when she's darn good and ready.

"You know, Big Boy, you were hot gossip after the party," Gram continued. "If the jury pool was comprised of Morningside residents, you'd skate." She made a whizzing noise.

"Thank you, that makes me feel so much better."

I almost poked Pryce, a reminder that sarcasm wasn't very nice, but didn't want Gram to see me.

The three of us trekked up to the restaurant, where I approached the hostess's desk and gave Avery's name. I'd called ahead and requested a table on the patio, hoping that would give us some privacy. There was no one waiting to be seated, so I left the names of the women we were expecting. The three of us followed as the hostess led the way to the table and set down the menus.

"Fun, fun, fun." Gram rubbed her hands together.

Pryce and I were behind her, and he rolled his eyes. "I'm sitting with you?"

"You're my dear, sweet brother, visiting from... somewhere," I said.

"Next time, and I say that because I know there will be one, we're going over every facet of the so-called plan before we set foot outside the house," Pryce said in a testy tone.

"We're here now, so... I figure it'll all come together once we meet the women and know what we're dealing with."

"As a top-notch CEO, is that how you would approach a business problem?" Pryce asked.

"Of course not." I grinned at him. "These last-minute jaunts of ours have been fun, and so has not having every angle worked out. Now I just hope I don't regret my lack of preparation."

"Flying by your designer heels will build character." Gram hooted. "As is learning to be a character."

"So there." Pryce leaned forward and brushed my lips with a kiss.

"Enough of the kissy business. If he's your brother... Ick." Gram followed up with a sound effect. "Who needs a drink?" Her hand shot in the air. "I'll take a double."

"Oh no you won't," Pryce said. All that was missing was a finger-shake. "In case you've forgotten, you're driving. Unless you agree to take an Uber, you can sugar up with a soda."

Gram wrinkled her nose. "I'll just have to wait until I get home to get my sauce on."

Two women, who I recognized as Millie and Olive from the pictures I'd forwarded myself from Avery's phone, were bearing down on us. They were so similar looks-wise that they could've passed for sisters—strained smiles, short grey bobs, and colorful sundresses. I tapped Pryce's leg and nodded in their direction. He gave a silent heads up to Gram. I got the introductions mixed up, introducing Pryce as Gram, and calling Gram Walker. Grey wouldn't be happy when he learned that I'd used his last name. But it turned out to be an icebreaker that had us all laughing.

"You brought your grandmother, how sweet," Olive said, but both women looked relieved. "I want to thank you for inviting us. We've heard such good things about this restaurant that it was impossible to pass up the invitation."

"I felt the same way. When I heard we'd be meeting here, no way could I pass it up." Gram moved her chair closer to the women, and they started chatting it up about places they'd been and things they had in common. The tension lines eased from the women's faces.

Pryce squeezed my hand under the table.

When the server came to take our order, Gram encouraged them to get whatever they wanted and also put in a dessert order to take home. She ordered her favorite, key lime pie, to take with her.

I picked up the dessert menu and set it in front of the women. "Better decide now, as they tend to sell out."

"Oh, we couldn't." Millie waved me off.

"Nonsense. Later, you'll be happy that you did," I assured her.

The server took our order, and when she left, Gram went back to chatting with the women as if they were old friends making up for lost time. You wouldn't have known that Pryce and I were sitting at the table except for the occasional sidelong glance. Gram kept up a steady stream of chatter until the food arrived. Everyone was happy with their choices, the ladies oohing over how yummy every bite was.

Once the plates were cleared and our drinks refilled, Gram's tactics changed, though her demeanor remained friendly as she took control of the turn the conversation took. "How long have you been living in that building?"

"For years now," Olive said. "Millie and I met out by the pool, and it wasn't long before we realized we had a lot in common and became fast friends."

"When a two-bedroom became available and going halfsies on it would be less than what we were paying for smaller units, we snapped it up," Millie said. "We got lucky—an investor bought the unit we currently live in and was looking for a stable renter. The other advantage is it was a long-term guaranteed lease."

"The building started out as rentals only, and then came the decision to sell the units individually. Most weren't prepared to buy and moved out," Olive said. "Though there are still a few rentals, most are owner-occupied. It's been a couple of years since the change, and it's ridiculous what some are paying for rent on the rare occasions there's an available unit."

"I say we cut through the bull and get down to business," Gram said abruptly, startling the two women. "Before we proceed any further, I need assurances that you two can keep what we're about to say secret. If you think that'll be an issue, no problem—we can take our desserts and go home."

"We were assured of anonymity during the phone call, so of course we'd have to keep our traps shut," Millie said. Olive nodded.

"I know these two really well." Gram's eyes swept over Pryce and me. "Her more than him, but still, I say that to let you know that I trust them both."

Pryce nudged me, *What's she doing?* on his face.

Errrr… I wanted to yell, *Crash imminent.* I pasted on a smile. "I think we should talk about any change of plans first." Now all eyes zeroed in on me.

"That train sailed," Pryce whispered. The women didn't appear to have heard him.

"What Rella really wants to know is if there's anything that you can share about Lili Ford. Even if it doesn't seem important, that can be sorted out later. The smallest bit of minutia may be all it will take to clear Pryce." Gram beamed and nodded at the women.

"Who?" Olive asked, staring between me and Gram.

"I'm sure the name you gave me was Avery; that's what I wrote down." Millie pulled a piece of paper out of her pocket and glanced at it. "Says so right here." She held it up.

"It's kind of a long story, but I can shorten it up so we're not here all day." Gram chuckled.

From the pressure on my thigh, Pryce didn't appreciate her finding this humorous.

"My other granddaughter, Avery, came up with this hokey story…" Gram laid out the whole writer/author scam.

I felt like a deer in the headlights and didn't dare peek at Pryce to see if he was feeling the same.

"She did it to help clear this man of murder, which I assure you he didn't commit," Gram continued.

Pryce groaned, and again, I was the only one to hear it.

"How do you know he didn't do it?" the two women asked at the same time and in the same whisper. They turned their full attention on Pryce, checking him out.

"You'd recognize him if it weren't for that dumb stache." Gram turned up her nose.

Pryce removed the glasses, since Gram was now squinting at them and, if I had to guess, was about to make fun of them too.

"How? Easy," Gram said with a snort. "Pryce had no reason to kill the woman; they weren't even a couple at the time. That stupid woman left him — at the altar, no less — and had already flown back to the states. Walking on the beach, he met Rella here and instantly knew that Lili had done him a favor, and they're living happily ever after." She feigned a swoon.

Pryce's lips quirked.

I leaned forward to stop Gram from divulging anything more personal. "I don't want you to think that you're under any obligation to answer questions, especially since I was less than truthful. If you want to leave, I'd understand. We all would." Gram would flip, but I wasn't asking her.

The two women turned to one another and communicated silently, shrugging a couple of times. "It's the most fun we've had in a while, despite the awkwardness of the last few moments," Millie said.

"What is it you want to know about Lili?" Olive asked. "We may not be the best ones to answer your questions, as we weren't friends by any stretch. Though we did have several conversations with her in passing."

"Lili and Daniel purchased their unit and have lived there two years," Millie said. "They let everyone believe that they were married, and it came as a big surprise when more than a few articles after her death claimed that she'd planned to marry someone else. We'd seen her a few days previous, and not a peep that they'd divorced."

"I used to see Daniel going for a run every morning," Olive said. "After Lili's death, he didn't come out of his house for several days. Shortly after the funeral, we took over a casserole, and he was falling-down drunk. Scared me, and we didn't waste time getting back home."

"None of this makes any sense. She was going to marry you?" Millie's brows went up as she zeroed in on Pryce. "Not to be mean, but Daniel and Lili appeared to be very much in love, always walking hand in hand. Laughing. Smiling. There wasn't a single noise complaint, unlike the neighbors on the other side, where the cops showed up several times, and every time, they insisted it was all a misunderstanding." She rolled her eyes. "Thankfully, they moved."

"You know…" Olive lowered her voice. "We were surprised that none of the neighbors were invited to the funeral. The only reason we knew about it was that I read her obituary online and called and verified the time and date, not realizing it might be invitation only. When we got there, the greeter asked our names and, after he checked the list, said, 'Must have been an oversight.' Neither of us corrected him."

"The poor turnout was kind of sad, considering that Lili had an outgoing personality. There were only two other guests, both women we'd seen visiting on several occasions," Millie said.

"Do you know anything about them?" Gram asked.

"Lili told us that they were all flight attendants who worked for the same airline," Millie said. "Olive and I saw the two in uniform on several occasions, but never Lili. Although we did see her rolling a suitcase out to the parking lot a few times. She'd quip 'short flight,' and we wouldn't see her for a week or more. We didn't have the kind of relationship where we could ask anything more than superficial questions."

"There was another woman who came around quite frequently, though she didn't attend the funeral," Olive said. "I remember her because she almost ran me down in the parking lot one day. Miss Leadfoot slowed and rolled down her window, shouted 'Watch where you're walking,' and off she went."

"I remember that, and for that reason, I didn't want to tell you that she's been staying with Daniel since Lili's death. I've seen her coming and going, but never the two of them together," Millie told her friend. Olive grimaced.

The desserts were boxed and delivered to the table.

"I want to thank you for agreeing to this sit-down," I said, smiling at the two women.

"This has been a lot of fun." Millie patted Gram's hand. "Nice to meet you."

"This might be our only chance to eat here, since it's too pricey for us," Olive said.

I pulled business cards out of my pocket and handed them to the women. "If you think of anything else, you can call anytime."

"Do you have another of those?" Gram asked.

I handed her one, and she scribbled on the back of the card and handed it to Millie. "You can always call me."

Millie and Olive were clearly excited by the prospect of getting together with Gram again.

We stood, and Gram had a few private words for the women. They then approached Pryce, leaned in, and whispered a few words.

He laughed and winked at them, picking up the to-go boxes and carrying them out to their car.

I walked Gram to her car and hugged and kissed her. "You were great in there, and I'm happy I had the foresight to invite you."

"I told them that if they had news to share, they better call me," Gram said in her bossy tone. "They got a kick out of that one. They're as nosey as I am, but shy about admitting it."

Pryce and I waited until the women pulled away from the curb before getting in the car. I u-turned and went in the opposite direction.

"What were you chatting about with the ladies?" I asked.

"They wished me the best with the trial and hoped I got off. I told them that if anyone else came snooping around, my advice was to feign ignorance. They got lucky with you, and it might not hold a second time."

"Good advice. The same could be said for us." I headed toward home.

"When Gram takes charge…" Pryce shook his head. "A couple of times, I wondered why I was there but sucked it up and pasted on a smile."

"Felt the same way."

"About the only interesting thing to come out was the woman who's living with Daniel. Wonder who she is and how she figures in," Pryce mused.

"Isn't it a little quick for someone to move in? I know that some people can't be alone, but isn't it a little soon?"

"It would make Avery happy if you were to sic her on uncovering the identity of the woman. It's a given, since she loves to snoop, that she'll be ecstatic to have another person to run down."

"That's a good idea. If anyone can get the information, it's her. I'll pose my questions to her and see if she can come back with any answers," I said.

"Not only did Lili have me fooled, she had a whole other life I knew nothing about and was a master at keeping me from finding out. Another interesting person to question would be Daniel. I'd like to know if he had any clue about her busy life."

"You trusted her." I squeezed his hand. "You didn't have any reason to believe she wasn't who she seemed to be. I can't imagine finding out, after getting married, that your partner isn't who you thought they were."

"Thus far, we've uncovered a couple of people who might've had a motive… but to kill her?"

"Another question for Avery: what was Lili's relationship with Daniel? Another mark?" I asked, shocked. "If Lili was already married to him, she'd risk a bigamy charge if she was found out. What a mess that would've been for you. It doesn't make sense for her to have waited until minutes before the ceremony to take off."

"If there's a husband lurking in the shadows, wouldn't he have a better motive than the one assigned to me?" Pryce asked in disgust. "I'm going to ask Cruz if the police have any other persons of interest. Probably not, since they charged me, and there's been no mention of continuing to investigate."

Chapter Eighteen

It had been a couple of days since our lunch with Millie and Olive, during which time, we shared everything we learned with Avery. It surprised me that we hadn't heard back from her, and I expected the door to fly open any minute and for her to regale us with whatever she'd found out. But so far — silence.

Pryce and I sat side by side at the big dining table on the balcony, clicking away on our laptops, sifting through the latest that our respective offices had sent over, both of us dealing with business that we hadn't given our full attention, since we'd gotten caught up in checking out the beach and finding a new restaurant.

I hadn't told Pryce that donations were down due to all the bad publicity. I'd make sure that none of the charities I supported would suffer, and I was sure it was only temporary. A fundraising dinner was rapidly approaching, and it wouldn't be good for contributions if I weren't there to schmooze. I wanted him to be my date but also didn't want him to feel like he was on display. Since I wasn't the sneak-around type, I'd tell him about the event and let him decide.

Pryce's phone rang, and after a quick look at the screen, he answered. He listened intently, scrunching up his nose, and a good minute went by with him saying nothing. "You're full of it! If you think I'm knuckling under to extortion, you've got the wrong man. I suggest you lose my number." He hung up and immediately placed a call.

What the heck?

"That was an interesting call." Pryce flashed the screen at me so I'd know he called Grey. After exchanging greetings, he said, "A man just called, claiming to have proof that I didn't kill Lili."

Wish I could hear both sides of the conversation.

"Claims to know two people that witnessed Lili's murder, and for the right price, he'd be willing to give them up." Pryce laughed grimly. "He also claimed that the reason these people haven't come forward is they're afraid to get involved."

I gasped. *They'd let an innocent man go to jail?*

Pryce turned to me with a shake of his head, *I can't believe this* on his face. "The caller claimed to be willing to part with the information for a mere 100K."

How could Pryce know it wasn't a con before shelling out the money?

"Told him that I didn't do extortion. Then, my anger getting the better of me, I hung up. I'm thinking now I should've played the game. The last thing I heard him say was, 'Think about it.'" Pryce put the phone on speaker so he could scroll through the screen and read off the number. "I'll wait to hear back." He hung up and tossed the phone on the table.

I looped my arm around his and pulled him into a side hug.

"The caller was cocky, certain I'd jump at his offer," he said into the top of my head.

"His parting comment sounds like you haven't heard the last of him. When he does call back, demand some proof that the information he's got is worth that kind of money."

"Basically the same thing Grey said. Avery was in hearing distance, and he called out the number to her, told her to hustle on the trace. I heard laughter, which was probably Seven. He said he'd call back the second Avery locates a name. But if the caller knows anything about electronics, he'll have removed the battery as soon as he hung up."

"Let's hope he's not smart and keeps calling, making it easier for Avery to track his location."

"Grey told me to answer all calls, and when I don't recognize the number, hit the record button."

"You recognize the voice?" I asked. Pryce shook his head in frustration.

No clue what else to suggest. Noticing his empty mug, I grabbed it, went into the kitchen, and filled it with coffee. I'd had enough and opted for iced tea. I took them both back outside and set them on the table.

"A wife who can read my mind." Pryce winked at me.

I sat next to him and opened my laptop, then picked up his phone, found the number, and typed it into the search bar. It was worth a try. But nothing. "Could it be someone you know? I'm wondering how they got your number."

"I didn't recognize the voice. But wouldn't it suck if it was someone I know well?"

"Yes, it would," I commiserated. "The big question is do they really have information or is it a money grab?"

We both sat in silence. I stared at my laptop, hoping for an answer to pop up. Pryce had closed his and stared out at the water. I wanted to say something that would take away the deep lines in his forehead.

A loud banging echoed out to the balcony.

"I liked it better when my friends used their keys. A knock that sounds like there's an elephant banging on the door is unsettling." I looked over my shoulder, wondering if they'd actually wait for me to open it. "If it's good news, I won't be so annoyed."

Pryce stood. "Quick wager as to who our guest turns out to be? Or guests?"

"If it's Avery and she comes bearing information, I won't hit her up for repairs to the door." I chuckled.

Pryce laughed on his way to the door.

It was hard to point the finger at who was doing the banging, since all four of our friends came trooping out to the balcony, drinks in hand, and sat down. I'd thought they were at the office. Guess we weren't the only ones working from home. It was a perfect sunny day for it.

Avery was the only one to show up with her laptop. She flipped open the lid the minute she sat down. "The number was a burner, and whoever it was was smart enough to toss it in the ocean or some other non-trackable option."

"That's disappointing." I'd hoped for a little stupidity to make it easier to track the extorter. He had to know that what he was attempting was a felony; probably the reason for the caution.

Seven nudged Avery. "Pitch your idea."

"I'll put a tracker on Pryce's phone and monitor the calls," Avery said.

Grey cleared his throat.

"I'm supposed to out myself." She glared at Grey. "There are already trackers on the rest of our phones and cars. I haven't had any reason to start snooping into who's calling whom. I can add the same tracker to Pryce's phone."

Pryce handed over his phone. "Good idea."

"I agree, and if you hadn't bugged mine already, I'd be handing it over." I grinned at her. "If I didn't trust you, I'd have to beat you up."

Pryce's brows went up. "Have you ever been

in a fistfight? I can't quite picture it."

"Nooo." The subject had come up before, and it'd turned out that none of us had ever duked it out. "It's worrisome that the caller knew how to get in touch with Pryce."

"Seven and I talked about it and are in agreement that the next time this guy calls, you should set up a meeting, and we'll surprise him by showing up," Grey said.

"I'll come along to take pictures. You know, in case he gets away." Avery bubbled with excitement. "I can do it all from the car with Seven's super camera."

"Gets away." Seven snorted, conveying *not happening*.

"Then what? Call in the cops?" I grimaced at the thought of those headlines.

"We're keeping our options open," Grey hedged.

That was nice and vague. I squeezed Pryce's leg. I wasn't opposed to any of their tactics; I just didn't want anyone to get hurt.

"How long do you think it will be before the caller makes contact again?" Pryce asked.

"If he's in desperate need of money, it'll be soon," Seven said. "So be sure to answer all your calls."

Chapter Nineteen

The unidentified caller didn't keep Pryce waiting for long. He called back the next morning while we were sitting outside, trying to decide what kind of trouble we could get into. Interestingly, the call came from the same number as before.

Pryce flashed me the phone screen before answering. "I need to know exactly what I'm purchasing, and I want proof that I'm not being scammed." After a pause, he said, "I'll be waiting," and hung up. The caller immediately sent a text. "Forwarding the recording to Grey." He then hit the play button and listened to the short conversation.

"You want the evidence to prove your innocence or not?"

I leaned forward and listened carefully. Not a voice I recognized, but he sounded young.

On the recording, Pryce made his demand for proof, and the extortionist must have been expecting it because he responded quickly. *"Give me a couple of minutes."*

"Be interesting to see what the guy sends over. Grey told me not to hold my breath—chances are high it won't be anything useful," Pryce said, his annoyance level visibly through the roof.

I patted his hand. I agreed with Grey, but Pryce didn't need to hear that.

It didn't take long, so Mystery Man must've been prepared. Pryce's phone dinged with an incoming text and then dinged again. I scooted over next to him. He opened the text and pulled up a picture of a man, his face in shadow, not clear enough to make an ID even if you knew the identity going in.

The next message was a few seconds of a recording. "I'm going to kill you…" a male voice neither of us recognized said. A loud rush of water in the background. Pryce listened a couple of times.

"The only thing that proves is that the voice isn't yours," I said. "Are we supposed to believe that the man in the picture and the one in the recording are one and the same? And even if we knew that, how does that prove your innocence?"

"This is a con, and whoever's behind the phone call is an amateur." Pryce's phone rang, and this time, he hit the speaker button.

"Obviously I couldn't show you everything I had, or why would you pay?" Mystery Man snickered. "The pictures I have are crystal clear and make the killer easy to identify."

I half-expected Pryce to laugh at the man but knew that wasn't the plan.

"Spell out what you want," Pryce said,

shaking his head.

"One hundred thousand big ones. And make it cash. You've got two days to get it together. I'll call back with the drop place and time."

"How the heck am I supposed to get that kind of cash together in so short a time?" Pryce demanded.

"Not my problem. Think of the money you'll save on lawyer bills." He hung up.

Pryce shot off texts to Avery and Grey.

Avery called back within a couple of minutes. "Dude's slipping; he didn't take the battery out or whatever he did before. I was able to track the purchase to a store in the outdoor marketplace. I'll snag Seven, and we'll go check out the place and find someone we can buy information from. Better us than you. You don't want to be seen anywhere around the area." She hung up.

"Let's hope our mystery man doesn't resort to violence when he finds out he's been double-crossed and is facing down Grey and Seven," I said. No telling how a cornered person would react.

Grey called, and he and Pryce talked. It was a short conversation.

"Seven was also on the call. One thing we all agree on — this guy is amateur hour, no clue what he's doing," Pryce said. "Makes the guys think he's hard up for money."

"Now what?" I asked. "How do we meet his demands? No bank is going to hand over that kind of money without a lot of questions. And if this guy gets his hands on the cash and gets away, it's a lot of money to be out."

Pryce got up, retrieved his briefcase, and withdrew an envelope. "Grey dropped this off." He turned it upside down and ten stacks of hundreds slid onto the footrest.

"He just happened to have this kind of cash lying around and was willing to hand it over?" I picked up one of the stacks and gently thumbed through it.

He reached back into his briefcase, pulled out a lone hundred-dollar bill, and handed it to me. "Compare this to one of those." He pulled one out and handed it over. "At first glance, they pass as the real deal. The one from the payoff is fairly realistic, and it would take a closer inspection to know it's phony money—prop money, to be exact. Grey suggested putting a real hundred on the top."

I held it up. It looked realistic, but Pryce was right—there were clear indicators that it was phony.

"Grey figures that our caller, once he's ready to go, will get back to us with last-minute instructions."

"I'm going in the all-girl car." I almost laughed as his brows bunched. "Don't even think that I'm going to sit home like a good wifey. I promise that I won't be getting up in the action, but I want to watch what goes down firsthand." I ignored him shaking his head at me. "One of my purchases from the spy store was several of those pens that record everything. No more borrowing from anyone. When the call comes in, we each take one."

"You super-swear promise that you won't risk your safety at any time?"

I held up my right hand. "Easy-peasy promise."

Chapter Twenty

Like clockwork, Mystery Man called two days later at almost the same time.

Pryce assured him he was ready to go. "Just know..." he barked, hitting the record button and then the speaker. "Before I hand over this envelope of cash, you're going to have to show me exactly what you have. If this is to screw with me, I'm not paying. Got it?"

I'd grabbed a manila envelope from the office for the money—there was plenty of room for it and the envelope itself wouldn't attract attention.

"No worries. You'll be a satisfied customer." The man laughed.

"Where are we meeting?" Pryce demanded.

"Bosco's coffee. Ten o'clock. It's at the far end of the marketplace, and I'll grab a table outside. If you're more than ten minutes late, the deal's off, and I won't be calling again."

"How will I know it's you?"

"I'll have on a 'Beautiful Alaska' baseball cap." He laughed again, the joke something only he knew. "One more thing—bring anyone, and it's possible you'll catch a stray bullet." He hung up.

Pryce sent out texts, then jumped up and

pulled me to my feet, and we didn't waste a second in running out the front door. The caller hadn't left us a lot of time to get to the drop-off spot. Harper and Avery flew out of their own doors and met us at the elevator, and we rode down to the garage together.

"The guys are on the way over from the office and should get to the marketplace ahead of us," Harper said. "It's a good thing we aren't all leaving from here—this way, we don't have a line of cars pulling out at the same time."

I gave Pryce a quick kiss. "Be damn careful." He hopped in his SUV and hightailed it out of the garage.

The three of us piled into Harper's SUV. Avery, in the front, had her laptop open and was tracking Pryce's location.

"Grey enlisted more muscle—Bosco's will be surrounded," Harper said as she cruised through the streets. "Whoever this is isn't going to get away. The only problem I see is if enough of a scene is created that the police get called. Then what? I wasn't in on the meeting where the guys talked about how they hoped it would all play out."

"I've been ordered to stay in the car. What about you two?" I asked.

"Oh yeah," both answered.

"These pen cameras were a great find," I said to Avery, thinking of the one I knew Pryce had in his shirt pocket. I opened the tracker app on my phone and saw that he'd just arrived at the marketplace.

Harper knew the streets well and quickly pulled into the last entrance and found a parking spot with a clear view of Bosco's, which turned out to be a drink cart. No wonder I hadn't found a website for it. There were three small tables with chairs and a bench; that last must have been the prime spot, as it was filled with three older women.

Pryce had parked in the middle of the lot and was now weaving through the cars to get to the mall. He grabbed a drink and claimed one of the tables, one arm anchoring the envelope.

We'd never talked about what to do if Mystery Man pulled out the money for closer inspection. Probably a moot point, since by that time, he'd be surrounded. "My heart's racing a mile a minute," I said, phone in hand so I could see and hear everything Pryce was witnessing. Occasionally, I scoped out the area in an attempt to locate all the WD guys, but wherever they were, they didn't stand out.

"Check this out." Avery pointed through the windshield.

From the far side of the courtyard, a cocky-looking twenty-something strutted up to the table and attempted to grab the envelope.

Pryce's leg flew out, and the guy landed on the concrete. He leaned down into the man's face. "You first. Hand it over."

The guy stood, rubbed his hands down his shorts, and sat down. "You need to calm down."

"You're not the one who called," Pryce said in an accusatory tone.

Mr. Cocky ignored him, pulled out his phone and scrolled across the screen, then handed it over. "There's three images there. Forward the information to yourself." He pulled a folded sheet out of his pocket and set it on the table. "This is the information you're expecting."

"I'll have a look first."

As the guy handed the phone over with one hand, he grabbed the envelope with the other, jumped up, and ran down a row of mall shops. He didn't appear to notice the two oversized men on his tail.

"It was all a scam," Pryce said in disgust as he scrolled through the phone. "Not that I'm surprised, but I'd hoped for useful information. Tell Avery I'm forwarding it." Avery's phone pinged, so done deal. He unfolded the piece of paper the guy left behind. "Blank." He shoved his chair back, trashed his cup, and followed the same path as the runner.

"WD guys have the runner in their sights," Harper said.

I checked my phone screen, but Pryce hadn't caught up yet.

"Local cops have him in custody," Avery announced.

"Didn't know that law enforcement was going

to be involved." I wondered if Pryce knew.

"Seven recruited a friend of his that's still on the force to take this guy down," Avery said. "If it's valid information, then the cops need to be involved so it'll hold up in court. If it isn't, what the guy did was a crime either way."

"Now what?" I asked.

"Runner is being taken to the local precinct for questioning. The guys are following, as they need to give their statements," Harper informed us.

I'd just realized that she had on an earpiece and was privy to everything that went down. "Pryce didn't plan on leaving his car here, and I don't have a set of keys." Hint, hint.

"No worries, I'll get it home." Harper got out and opened the back hatch. Removing the carpet, she opened a built-in box and removed a slim jim, then tossed me her keys. "No speeding around in my ride." Minutes later, she was behind the wheel of Pryce's SUV and headed out of the parking lot.

"Okay, I'm impressed by Harper's tricks, but why couldn't I be the one to drive Pryce's car?" I asked, having moved to the front seat. I sent off a quick text to Pryce: *Your car is headed home. Get a ride or call me.*

"Harper likes the thrill of boosting a car and driving off," Avery said with a grin. "I pestered her to teach me jacking techniques and I strived to be a good student. Then Seven found out and put his oversized foot down. He pointed out that if caught, I'd be hauled straight to jail. No thanks, once is enough."

That was an experience I didn't want to have. "I wish we knew what was going on."

"Seven turned off the microphone, so they're probably talking to the cops or at the station," Avery said. "We'll know everything that happened—the guys are good at remembering every bit of detail, since they know that's the way I like it. Hate the condensed version."

"Next to you and Harper, I feel like a one-trick chick. Not totally boring, but close." We laughed.

Chapter Twenty-One

It was several hours before the guys got home, and they were tired and a tad grouchy. Harper called dibs on being hostess, declaring that food was a necessity. I'd raided all our refrigerators, grabbing an assortment of drinks and putting them in an ice-filled enamelware bucket. Good thing, because the first thing the guys reached for after claiming a kiss was a beer. Avery had already called in an order for Mexican food, and it was soon delivered. We were in agreement that it was one of the few choices that wouldn't taste like paste if it had to be reheated.

We steered the guys out to the patio, where everything was set up, and proceeded to feed them and ply them with alcohol until their faces lost their intensity and we'd gotten a few laughs out of them.

In the warmth of the afternoon sun, we sat facing the ocean, the waves washing up against the shore. Drinks were refilled, and we moved to more comfortable chairs, all eager for details.

"Whoever's the brains behind this scam, they made sure that if a trap was sprung, they wouldn't be caught up in it," Grey said.

"Turns out that Dillon, the kid who confronted Pryce, is just out of high school," Seven said. Pryce shook his head. "A complete stranger approached him and hired him to retrieve an envelope and bring it back, and not only did that arrangement not raise red flags but Dillon didn't ask any questions."

"Wish we'd had a better way to handle this than involving the cops, but we needed the evidence to be admissible," Grey said in frustration. "Turned out there wasn't any."

"I arrived on the scene as the cops were loading Dillon in the back of a cop car," Pryce said.

"The mastermind was close by, I'm sure, secreted in some corner, watching everything go down and breathing a huge sigh of relief," Seven said in disgust. "The three of us went to the police station, leaving a couple of WD's guys behind to blend in and keep a lookout. They stayed for about an hour and reported that they didn't pick up anything out of the ordinary. If Mystery Man stuck around, he played it cool, not bringing attention to himself. Our guys think whoever it was left at the first sign of trouble."

"Did you get to hear Dillion's story?" Avery asked.

"Not from him directly but through my friend," Seven said.

"Dillion told the cops he was approached by a stranger, and for fifty dollars, all he had to do was drop off the phone and bring back the envelope," Grey related. "Another fifty when the job was done. Interestingly, Dillion was under a time restriction and had to hustle. The final warning from the man was, 'Screw me, I'll find you and get even,' And still not one question from the kid or a warning going off in his head to run."

"Pretty damn stupid," Seven agreed. "Our cop friend thinks the kid knew it was a dodgy offer but got caught up in the excitement and didn't want to pass up a hundred bucks for what he thought would be five minutes of work."

Avery, who'd grabbed her laptop and been clicking away, now looked over the top. "The images that you sent from your phone, the ones the guy wanted big money for…" She turned her laptop around. "The first two are headshots of B-list actors." She pointed to their mugs. "The third was a shot of a piece of paper with the supposed addresses of these men, and they're also bogus. Both come up as empty fields."

His voice flat with disgust, Pryce said, "My phone rang while I was at the police station. At Grey's urging, I answered. Recognized the voice. He did all the talking, and the message was short: 'You're stupid. Now you're going to hang.' Handed over the number to the cops after a quick text to Avery. They were skeptical that it would yield any information. Avery had already verified that it was a burner and no longer giving off a signal."

"How did Dillon do under questioning, or did he keep his mouth shut?" Harper asked.

"They put him through several hours of questioning, which Dillon answered in precise detail," Grey said. "He gave a description of the man who hired him, though it's fairly generic. It was the consensus of the detectives that he was telling the truth, so he was released with an admonition to make himself available when they called."

"You're not going to like this part," Seven said to Pryce. "The cops think it was just a scam, not anyone with legit information. Most likely, it was someone who followed the case and paid for your contact information, thinking you were an easy mark."

"Does that happen often?" I asked. Everything I was learning proved that I was still pretty naïve.

Seven nodded. "There's always someone reporting that they've been scammed, some more sophisticated than others. Often, the cops are able to catch up to the perpetrator. They got a laugh off the prop money, saying that the stuff shows up in stores occasionally, even though it's blatantly fake and almost impossible to pass off as real."

"Based on your experience as ex-detectives…" Avery pointed to Grey and Seven as though we didn't know who she meant, which elicited chuckles. "Does our extorter make another attempt or move on to the next mark?"

"Now that Mystery Man knows that the cops are involved, I say he's moving on. Unless he's a bigger dumbass than we think he is," Grey said. Seven nodded.

"I've got a little news. Grey and Seven already know and said I could be the one to tell." Avery grinned at them. "Turns out Daniel Stone was a bigamist until Lili died."

"So she really was married to him." Pryce leaned back and stared up at the ceiling. "Was there anything about the woman that wasn't fake?"

"Lili did file for divorce last year, and maybe she thought it was a done deal," Avery informed us.

"Just one more thing I didn't know about Lili. She never mentioned having been married. In fact, she made a point of saying that her marriage to me would be her one and only."

"Who's his other wife?" Harper asked.

"Amy Peters—technically the second wife and now the only one. I'm saying that because I haven't found records of any other wives," Avery said, clearly pleased with her investigative abilities. "I'm going to ask Gram to find out from Mollie and Olive if Amy's the woman Daniel's living with."

"Have you run a background check on this Amy person?" I asked.

"Not yet. I'll get to it tonight."

"If you haven't already, would you forward a copy of everything you find to Cruz?" Pryce asked. "Not sure it'll be anything that could benefit me, but it can't hurt."

Avery beamed. "That gives me another opportunity to show off to Cruzer."

Chapter Twenty-Two

Running out of time, I finally fessed up to Pryce that I had a charity event I had to attend, as contributions had dropped and my appearance would go a long way to getting our biggest donors to be free with their checkbooks. I told him I'd understand if he didn't want to attend—I wasn't going to ask him to put himself on display and thought it needed to be his decision.

Pryce didn't hesitate. "I'm going. Maybe your guests will be awed by rubbing elbows with a killer; they might add an extra zero or two to their donations."

"You're not—"

"I think it's amazing, everything you do to raise money for disadvantaged women and children. Having been to a few of these functions, I'll just show them I can stick my nose in the air with the best of them."

I gave him a big hug. "You've got a couple of days to change your mind, and I'll understand if you bail."

"Not happening." Pryce leaned in and sealed it with a kiss.

* * *

Hot, hot, hot. Pryce was wearing a pair of black tuxedo pants and a white dress shirt, and I felt sexy by his side in a strapless black gown with a full skirt and a slit on one side that went past my knee. My blond hair was swept up off my neck, and I wore diamond earrings that Pryce had surprised me with.

"You look damn good." I straightened his tie and gave him a quick kiss for his patience.

"You're always beautiful, but tonight, you look amazing."

After a surprisingly quick drive, thanks to light traffic, we arrived at the Southernmost Winery just south of Miami. It was a large estate nestled in tropical foliage. The property, and the family that owned it, had quite a long history.

When I pulled up to the winery, luxury cars were lined up around the block, dropping off the wealthy of Miami who were willing to donate to a good cause.

As I came to a stop in the line of cars, Pryce entwined his fingers with mine. Bringing my hand to his mouth, he pressed his lips to the backs of my fingers. "Just watch, I'm going to charm these people; your donations will be higher than your last event." He leaned over and nibbled at my earlobe.

A horn blared behind us, and we shifted away from each other and followed another vehicle into the parking lot at a snail's pace. Once parked, I reached for the door handle, but Pryce grabbed my arm. He got out and came around, opened my door, and extended his hand to help me out. Then he took my arm and led me toward the entrance.

We entered an open courtyard and were surrounded by lush landscaping; water flowed freely in the manmade waterfalls, and overhead strings of lights illuminated the area. On both sides of the aisle that ran down the center of the courtyard, barrels of wine were stacked high, and several long bars were set up, bottles and glasses lined up on them.

"Since it's an amazing night—" I glanced up at the deep-blue sky, where stars glittered brightly. "—the wine-tasting portion will be outside, with dinner inside. Tonight's donations will go to fund several charities that help single women with children get back on their feet and build a life."

"From what I've seen so far, this is a pretty amazing place," Pryce whispered in my ear. "What would you like to drink?"

"White wine." I watched him head off to the bar, my eyes following his every step.

"Rella!" boomed Reilly Tanner, wife number six glued to his side. "Guess the gossip's wrong. You're looking good."

Reilly was a longtime contributor, and when he was in between wives, he used our functions to look for a lucky woman to become the next Mrs. Tanner. The man was totally full of himself — an outgoing personality that eclipsed everyone around him. I liked him anyway. He certainly had a type as far as wives went; I'd met the last three, and they were all cold and snotty.

"It's good to see you both," I said with a genuine smile that dimmed when the wife glared at me.

"Did you bring the murderer?" she asked snidely, looking around.

"Sweetheart." Reilly slung his arm around his wife's shoulders, *Well, did you?* on his face.

I noticed that he didn't introduce his wife; maybe he'd forgotten her name. Whatever was going on between then, her lips squeezed into a tight frown. Just then, Pryce reappeared at my side. "They were just asking if I brought the *murderer*."

"If you're talking about me, I haven't been convicted yet." He extended his hand, and the two men introduced themselves.

Once again, no introduction of Reilly's wife. Her expression morphed into a pout. "Rich people know how to buy their way out of trouble," she said in a knowing tone.

"We have every confidence that the truth will come out." I waved, looking over Reilly's shoulder; though they turned, they couldn't know there wasn't anyone to return the gesture. "It was great seeing you again. Grab yourselves a glass of wine. It's some of the best." I was prepared to tug Pryce away, but he was already pulling me away before they could respond. As soon as we were out of earshot, I said, "Where's our wine?"

"I was about to place our order, then turned and caught that guy ogling you and decided I needed your help in deciding which one to choose." Pryce led me toward the bar, where we each made our choice.

"Your first introduction went awkwardly. Are you ready to be introduced to the rest of the inquiring stares?" I asked. "I apologize in advance. Just because people have oodles of money doesn't mean they have any manners."

"Don't worry about me. I'll take my cue from Gram—if the question or comment is too ridiculous, I'll answer with something that makes no sense."

"Love it." We both laughed.

We made the rounds, and I made introductions, proud of the man by my side. Most showed no reaction; a few stared longer than normal. No more murderer questions, but a few awkward comments.

"So you're the one," one blue-haired woman said, eying Pryce and ignoring that my arm was linked in his.

"You're correct—I'm the lucky man married to this beautiful woman," Pryce said with a big smile.

The woman snorted. "Good one."

"I thought so." I smiled at her.

Thankfully, a couple of women from my office who'd met Pryce at the second wedding joined us, wanting to talk.

Just before dinner, I excused myself and went to the ladies' room. Staring in the mirror, I smiled at my flushed cheeks. The door opened, and I heard several female voices and quickly slipped into a stall, not wanting to make small talk. From the noise they were making, I guessed there to be at least four out there.

"Since when do murderers get bail?" one woman demanded.

"If I were the judge, I'd have let him out, but only if he came and stayed at my house," another giggled.

I rolled my eyes.

"Except your husband wouldn't go for that arrangement," a third voice sneered.

"That's probably the best Rella could do." The women snickered.

"Now that you mention it, I don't recall seeing her with a date before. Except that one man, but I heard she rented him." She laughed.

What was she talking about? Better yet, who? I always had a date, usually someone I had business dealings with who wanted to further their connections. Apparently, no one had made the connection that they were my dates, since it wasn't often that I brought the same man twice.

Equally tired of hiding and the snotty comments, I took a breath, pasted on a smile, and opened the door. "Hello, ladies. Hope you're enjoying yourself." I washed my hands, eyeing the women in the mirror and recognizing all of them. It didn't surprise me that none of them appeared embarrassed.

"Good to see you again," Reilly's wife said, insincerity in every word.

"Have a good time." I walked out, pleased that a couple of them had forgotten to close their mouths. I easily found Pryce, who was laughing. He introduced me to Jeff Cole, a banker his company had a business relationship with, and mentioned that they'd put together several deals. His wife joined us, and they were both friendly.

Eventually, we were called in to dinner. Pryce helped me to my seat. At our table at the front, I introduced Pryce to those he hadn't met, then told him, "Once I give my one-minute welcome speech, which I can cut to ten seconds, we can sneak out of here."

"What we're going to do is show the tongue-waggers that we're the perfect couple," Pryce whispered in my ear. "Ran into another associate and we shared a few laughs, which raised a few eyebrows, but after that, more than a couple of people wanted to be introduced, and that's a good sign."

I got a quick kiss from him before I made the way to the microphone to give my "Thank you for coming" speech, which I had memorized, and though tempted to shorten it, I didn't. The speech was met with applause, and my smile was genuine.

Chapter Twenty-Three

A week later, Pryce got a call from Cruz. His presence was required in court the next morning. The charges were being dropped, though it wouldn't be official until the judge banged his gavel.

We arrived early, easily found a parking space, and headed up the steps to the courthouse. Having been there a couple of times now, we knew where to go and rode the elevator to the third floor. Cruz was already there, speaking to an official-looking gentleman. We were steps away when the bailiff came out and unlocked the door. The man Cruz had been talking to went into the courtroom, and the surrounding benches emptied as people filed inside. Spotting us, Cruz waited as we approached.

"The lab's been backed up and slower than usual, and it took this long to get all the test results back on Lili's murder. The great news is that neither your fingerprints nor your DNA were found inside the old boat or on anything else," Cruz told us. "One of the previous owners came forward, and it turns out the boat's had several owners since you owned it and was abandoned by the last one."

I side-hugged Pryce, and he tightened his hold.

"Unfortunately, there was no footage to be garnered from the security cameras, as they hadn't been in working order in a long time, so they weren't able to make an ID of anyone entering the dock area. The cops talked to boat owners down there, but no one saw anything, which is a familiar story." Cruz nodded to someone passing by. "There was tissue found under Lili's fingernails. It belonged to a woman, but they weren't able to match it to anything on file. She was not only strangled but hit on the back of the head, and abrasions on her legs suggest that she was dragged. Another exculpating factor for you, since you could have picked her up."

"I knew there couldn't be any hard evidence, but it's great to have it confirmed." Pryce looked relieved.

"There were no eyewitnesses that cops uncovered. And no one has come forward to say they saw the two of you together after you left the island," Cruz said with a reassuring smile. "As a result, the prosecutor's dropping the case. They knew their motive was weak, since you'd already broken up, which I pointed out several times. We're first up, and the hearing will be short."

He motioned for us to follow him into the courtroom and for Pryce to join him at the defense table. I took a seat behind the defendant's table, and a man and woman sat down on the prosecution side. Next, the clerk showed up, and then the judge.

It didn't take long for the judge to call the courtroom to order. He wore a permanent scowl on his face while he heard from both sides. I realized I was holding my breath and reminded myself to breathe. Finally, Pryce was asked to stand, and the judge made it official.

I somehow refrained from yelling woo-hoo.

As the judge adjourned the hearing, Pryce and Cruz shook hands. I wanted to throw my arms around him but instead shook hands. Then Pryce linked his hand in mine, and we left the courtroom, breathing huge sighs of relief once we were clear of the building.

"No more coming back here," I said once we were back at the car. I wrapped my arms around Pryce in a fierce hug. "Now we go home and celebrate the good news. I'll order your favorites."

He was uncharacteristically quiet on the drive home, cruising over the Causeway on another picturesque day, the water, shades of vibrant blue, rippling along both sides. He finally broke the silence. "I want to thank you for standing by my side during this whole ordeal. Now that my court case is behind me, what about our marriage? Say the word, and I'll move back to Palm Beach. Whatever you want, I'll make it happen."

"Do you want a divorce?"

"Hell no," he said emphatically.

"Me neither. I do think we have a few things to figure out, but next week or next month. We're not in a hurry, are we?"

"I've been thinking…"

"Hmm… can't be good, since the lines on your forehead just caved inward."

Pryce rubbed his face.

I laughed. "Hang on." I hit the gas and took the exit toward home. "We need a walk on the beach."

Chapter Twenty-Four

That night, I made reservations for the six of us at Shark's, a local seafood restaurant, requesting a corner table on the outside patio and a bottle of champagne. Pryce thought it would be just the two of us, but I wanted to surprise him with a celebratory dinner. I'd told everyone casual tropical wear.

We easily found on-street parking less than a block from the restaurant, which was located on trendy Ocean Drive with a view of the white sandy beaches of the Atlantic. The restaurant had a low-key atmosphere and a reputation for fabulous food. I'd made certain that we would arrive after everyone else. The hostess escorted us to our table out on the patio, an area dotted with palm trees and wrapped in lights within an arm's reach of the sidewalk. Our friends saw us approach and waved.

Pryce pulled me closer and whispered, "What's going on?"

"Surprise," they called out.

He kissed my cheek, pulling out a chair for me. Our champagne glasses were filled, and we raised them as everyone offered their congratulations.

"What's next for you, now that you don't have the court case hanging over your head?" Grey asked Pryce.

He covered my hand with his. "We're still mulling over our options but keep getting sidetracked."

My cheeks burned, though I loved that sexy wink of his.

"Since you're in the *mulling* stage, let me make something clear," Harper said fiercely. "You are not moving Rella to Palm Beach. Whatever plan you come up with has to include staying right here."

"I second that." Avery waved the server over to take another drink order.

"You don't have to worry about me talking Rella into anything that she doesn't want to do. If that's even possible."

I squeezed Pryce's hand.

Our drinks were served and our order taken.

"I was about to out my beautiful Avery—" Seven eyed her with a wiggle of his brows. "—as having something up her sleeve, but her dress doesn't have them."

Harper and I grinned at her.

Avery made a face at Seven. "I'm not sure what the prosecutor's office plans to do about finding Lili's murderer, but I'd like to stay on the case. It's only right for someone to be brought to justice and your name completely cleared."

"In hindsight, I realize that my relationship with Lili was..." Pryce shook his head. "But I don't have any hard feelings and would like to see someone charged and not get off scot-free. But this also depends on how Seven feels about you continuing to poke around."

"I think this is where I point out that there's someone walking around who won't feel quite as comfortable now that there's no suspect about to go on trial," Grey said. "Highly doubt that they're happy with the recent turn of events. You or someone else goes poking around and the murderer gets wind of it, no one can predict how they will react. There's already one dead person; we don't want to add to the count."

"If you could promise not to go anywhere by yourself—" I zeroed in on Avery. "—and mean it..."

"How about I swear that if I discover anything interesting, the first thing I'll do is inform all of you? That way, you can offer your input."

Harper and I exchanged *sure she will* expressions. Avery would remember her promise only when she was miles away in hot pursuit, and it wouldn't slow her down. This topic was sure to start a fight based on the tight-lipped looks on the men.

"No more talk about the case," I interjected. "On to happier topics. Good news to share: I was worried about donations for our most recent fundraiser, but they matched our original projections. Also, the winery reported that their sales were through the roof, which made them happy. And not a single word of negative feedback."

"I meant to tell you that there was a writeup in the local 'Hot and Happening' section about your event," Harper said. "I think they just wanted an excuse to publish pictures of you and Pryce. They were good shots of both of you, and to their credit, they refrained from any lurid headlines. I'll forward it to you."

A woman thrust her head through a gap between two of the potted palm trees. "If it isn't the murderer," she squealed, loudly enough that passersby on the sidewalk slowed and, in some cases, stopped to stare. "Oh, that's right—he got off. Murdered his fiancée and moved on." She continued to squeal and jab her fingers in Pryce's direction, in case the starers weren't sure who she meant.

"If you don't leave, I'm calling the cops." Grey's fierce tone should have told her it wasn't an idle threat.

Seven shoved his chair back and stood. "Beat it."

The woman jumped back, then poked her head around the next palm tree, looking over the heads of the couple at the next table, who moved away from her. Her flinty brown eyes bored into Avery, who positioned her phone to get a better shot. "What the hell do you think you're doing?"

"If you're going to make an ass out of yourself, I want a video."

"Give me that." Her hand swiped out, but she was far enough away that she almost lost her balance and ended up hitting Seven's arm. "You broke my hand," she screamed.

"Nice try, sweets," Seven said, laughing at her. "Good thing we have video proof that didn't happen."

Grey held his phone up. "Don't say you weren't warned." He put it to his ear. "Yes, 911? I'd like to report…"

That got the woman moving. She stopped at every table as she continued down the sidewalk, informing the guests that there was a murderer in their midst and jabbing her finger towards our table. Her voice finally faded out, and at the far end, she waved her middle fingers at us.

Harper laughed. "That was fun."

Who the hell was that?

"I'm taking this as a sign that I should lie low for a while," Pryce said grimly.

"Nonsense," I said. "Even if you'd gone to trial and been found not guilty, there'd be some people that couldn't pass up the opportunity to cause a scene." I noticed Grey pocketing his phone. "Is it too late to cancel your call?"

"I never made the call. I figured going through the motions would be enough to send her on her way," Grey said.

Avery stared at her phone screen, replaying the video. "It took me a minute, but I finally recognized the woman. She's Amy Peters, Daniel's second wife."

Seven, who'd been scanning the sidewalk, sat down. "I kept my eyes on her as she disappeared down the street and didn't see her meet up with anyone. Or they were embarrassed by her behavior and moved on, not wanting to get caught up in the drama."

A man showed up at the table, introducing himself as the manager. "Is everything okay here?" He eyed us skeptically.

"That poor woman," I said in a sad tone. "She must have just been released from the hospital. She still had the ID bracelet on. Hope she gets the help she needs."

Everyone at the table backed up my outrageous lie with sympathetic expressions.

Whatever questions the manager had were cut off by the food arriving, and he watched as we were served.

"This looks and smell delicious," I said.

"Enjoy," he said, and off he went.

"One last bit of business—we've got an address for Amy, so why not go embarrass the hell out of her," I said to Avery.

"I'm coming along to watch," Pryce said.

Everyone laughed.

Talk was casual as we ate, the huge scene not affecting our appetites in the slightest.

Chapter Twenty-Five

We'd had a peaceful couple of days, during which Pryce and I worked from home and walked on the beach twice a day.

That morning, my phone rang early, which generally meant work. But when I picked it up off the nightstand and glanced at the screen, Harper's face smiled back at me. This couldn't be good news.

"I'm surprised you didn't just barge in and get me out of bed. Not feeling well?" I asked upon answering, rolling over to face Pryce.

"Avery and I had a bet, but since money wasn't mentioned, I suppose it technically isn't one."

I laughed. "What was it the two of you were trying to one-up each other on?"

"Who'll be the first to ferret out anything newsworthy. You know how it is when we have a little downtime." Harper chuckled. "Besides, Grey and Seven sat us down and had one of those squinty-eyed chats about barging in, suggesting, albeit nicely, that we knock it off."

"Pryce and I agree. And also agree that we won't be doing it either." I winked at him.

"Those older ladies you took to lunch, their apartment caught fire two nights ago."

I groaned. "That's awful."

"Luckily, firefighters were able to get it out quickly and the neighbors sustained only minimal damage."

"Are Millie and Olive okay?" I asked.

"Thankfully, they're fine. They weren't home at the time and have been cleared as suspects. Grey called a friend of a friend and found out that it was ruled arson."

"Arson? That makes no sense. Are you sure it wasn't something like leaving the stove on?" I pulled the phone away from my ear, gave Pryce a quick recap, then hit the speaker button so he could hear firsthand.

"No accident. The carpet in the dining room was doused with gasoline."

"Why would anyone do such a thing? Millie and Olive are older women and came off as harmless, not the type to stir up trouble. Though they were willing to contribute to a story about the murder, they were adamant about their names not being mentioned."

"Well…"

"There's more." I sighed. This call wasn't a good way to start the morning.

"Grey also found out that a few days before the fire, they got into a shouting match with two younger women out in the parking lot. By the time the cops arrived, the younger ones had sped off in an older model sedan, and no one could identify them. One of the neighbors reported hearing 'Keep your flaps shut' from the younger women, but the cops thought the witnesses weren't very credible."

"Hopefully, it didn't have anything to do with me taking them to lunch."

"Wondered the same thing," Harper said. "There's more. The HOA President inserted himself into the middle of the drama, bellowing for everyone to go back inside, and the cops told him to follow his own advice. Even after Millie and Olive insisted they didn't start anything, that they were the ones accosted, his parting comment was, 'If it happens again, I'll make sure your lease is terminated.'"

"Grey got all this information from the cops?" I asked.

"Mostly," Harper hedged. "I finagled a phone number for one of the residents and got a couple of questions answered, then hung up quickly before the tables got turned. Grey, who'd been listening, didn't think I found out anything newsworthy."

"I don't want to know." Why bother to ask how she got the number or knew about the fire? I knew she wouldn't answer. I did know that she had the skills to set up notifications for anything that could remotely affect one of her clients, which would come in handy in a situation like this.

"One more thing before you hang up on me." Harper sniffed. "According to my source, on the few occasions Mollie and Olive have returned to the property since the fire, not one of the residents has been friendly, when they were before. Now, not so much as a hello."

"Do you know where they're living?" I asked. "I know they're on a limited income, and if all they got out with was their purses, they're not going to have a lot of options."

"I can hear you thinking."

"I'm going to sic Gram on them; she can offer to help in her own pushy way. I know she won't take no for an answer. I'll gently remind her to treat them like she'd want to be treated if she were going through the same thing."

"You know this isn't your fault," Harper insisted.

"What if it was?"

"How would anyone find out that you met them?"

"Whether I'm responsible or not, I can certainly help them. My foundation assists people in need all the time, and they certainly qualify." I glanced at the clock. "Do you think Gram's awake this early?"

"She's up at the crack of dawn—annoys her to waste time sleeping until a more civilized hour." Harper laughed. "When I find out where Millie and Olive went, I'll let you know."

DEBORAH BROWN

"The three women exchanged numbers, so Gram can call them directly. I'm certain they'll be happy to hear from her."

"Keep me updated," Harper said and hung up.

I scrolled through my phone, found Gram's number, and called her.

"Maybe they were so excited by the lunch that they weren't able to keep it to themselves," Pryce suggested.

I held up my finger and pushed the speaker button.

"Must be important if you're calling this early," Gram chirped.

I recapped the details.

She gasped. "With rents the way they are, it's going to be hard for them to find a place on a fixed income."

"That's where you come in." I ignored her grunt. "I want you to get in touch with Millie and Olive and tell them you heard about the fire. Then you tell them about this apartment building owner you know that can get them a furnished unit for a song. Find out what they can afford, and I'll match that. Also, mention there's a special right now — first month free."

"Woah." Gram unleashed a long breath.

"One more thing, and the most important — you are not to mention my name."

"Why don't you ever want anyone to know the nice things you do? This one's a doozy." Gram clucked.

I didn't answer. No one understood that I didn't want or need acclaim for my every action. "I'll text you the address of the building and the manager's number so you can set up an appointment that's convenient for all of you. If you need anything, let me know."

We ended the call, and I called the manager of the building I had in mind. "Sorry to call so early." I explained what I needed.

After I hung up, Pryce said, "I'm learning more about you. I take it you own a building other than this one."

"My parents owned a few, and I've never had any reason to sell them. This particular property is located on the other side of the Causeway, close to where the women once lived, so they'll be familiar with the area."

"To most, it wouldn't occur to offer help, and here you've solved a problem the women have probably been stressing about since they came home and found they'd lost everything." Pryce brushed his lips across my cheek. "I can't imagine either of them doing anything that would provoke an act so vile. It could've ended in the whole building burning down and many more people homeless. Since it's been declared arson, my suggestion is that they not leave a forwarding."

"Even if they gossiped about anything and everything, what kind of person would set fire to someone's home?" I didn't expect an answer. "Avery will be happy because I'm going to ask her to pump Seven for information and run a check if any names come up. Wait until she finds out that Harper got the jump on her. I'm not surprised that she didn't waste time in getting someone to talk to her once she found out about the fire. Who knows what kind of story she fed them to get them to open up?"

"I don't know how those two manage to shake information out of people, and they're never the least bit embarrassed." Pryce chuckled.

"Speaking of… Avery's still trying to identify those two flight attendant friends of Lili's that Millie said were at the funeral. She wasn't happy to learn that there were other guests in attendance who didn't sign in." I knew she liked every question answered.

"You're thinking about something awfully hard."

"I'm going to have Gram ask Millie and Olive if the women who confronted them were Lili's friends and the same ones they saw at the funeral."

The bedroom door received a hefty push inward. Bruno stuck his head inside and looked around, then headed straight for the bed, resting his head on the mattress.

I rolled over and sat on the end of the bed. "I'll

make the coffee."

"And I get to feed Bruno?" Pryce laughed. "I've made inroads with your dog; he's stopped glaring at me like I'm an intruder." He scratched Bruno's head.

"That's because of the treats you sneak him when you think I'm not looking."

"It's working." He winked.

Chapter Twenty-Six

I was already running late when I pulled into the underground garage and parked, eager to get upstairs, kick off my shoes, and hopefully get a foot rub from my husband. Husband. That made me smile. We had plans for dinner at home and a movie. As I opened the door to the lobby, an arm snaked around me from behind, gripping me tight. My briefcase, purse, and keys scattered across the floor, and I was pushed against the wall, my face ground into the plaster. Panic set in as an unfamiliar voice hissed menacingly in my ear, "Bitch, you're coming with me." Definitely a man.

Hoping someone, anyone, would hear me, I opened my mouth to scream, but a wadded rag was shoved inside, the smell making me gag. I struggled to quell the fear, telling myself to breathe through my nose. He planted a fist to the side of my face, which exploded with searing pain. Nubby fingers tangled in my hair and dragged me to a nearby sedan. The man opened the back door and shoved me face down on the backseat, then snapped a pair of metal cuffs on my wrists.

"It would be a shame to shoot you, but if you try anything, you'll leave me no choice." The door slammed shut, another opened, and the locks were engaged. "Behave now," he shouted, and the car squealed forward. Turning my head, I tried to catch a glimpse of my abductor, since I'd barely gotten a look at the man before he hit me and didn't recognize the voice. It was a long shot, and now all I could see was the back of the seat. The interior reeked of cigarettes and body odor. It hadn't been cleaned for a long time, if ever. Feeling breathless, I dropped my head to take calming breaths.

How had I been kidnapped so easily from my own property? Hopefully, Avery'd had some reason to check the security feed and saw me being dragged off. Pryce was expecting me, as I'd called when I left the office. When I didn't show, what would he do? If he checked the garage, he'd see my car parked in its usual space. Before he got that far, though, he'd see the contents of my purse scattered on the ground. Both would be a big red flag.

Why was the man driving so recklessly? I hoped he'd attract the attention of the cops. More importantly, what did he want? I had to quiet the questions before they drove me crazy. He did say he didn't want to shoot me; hopefully that didn't mean he wanted to kill me another way, and hopefully, he'd let me go after he got what he wanted. Maybe this was a case of ransom, and he'd somehow been able to discover my net worth. If that was the case, so much for keeping a low profile. Until recently, the only times my name showed up on social media had to do with the charity functions I attended, but that changed when I married Pryce and the coverage became more salacious. Even though the charges had been dropped, there hadn't been another scandal for the reporters to move on to.

As the car slowed, then rocketed around a corner, and then a couple more, I rolled sideways, my head banging against the back of the seat, the torn upholstery scraping my cheek. I struggled to stay calm. Eventually, the car squealed to a stop. It was hard to tell how far we'd driven and no clue in which direction. We idled for several minutes before the engine cut off.

He got out, slamming the door. I didn't know how long I lay there before the door opened. Strong fingers gripped my ankles and hauled me across the seat and out of the car into an awkward half-stand. The heel of one of my shoes snapped, making me stumble, but he caught me before I hit the ground. Once on solid footing, I sucked in a deep breath and remained quiet.

He whirled me around. I barely stopped myself from screaming, blinking several times as I realized I was staring into the dark beady eyes of Daniel Stone.

"Go ahead, make a run for it; see what I do to

you." Daniel's fingers bit into my forearm, and I could almost feel the bruises forming as he marched me forward. "Try not to fall. I won't be a gentleman and catch you a second time." He chuckled. "Should you escape... When I recapture you, and I will, I'll teach you a painful lesson. Then..." He drew his finger across his neck, mimicking the noise.

I shivered, which he noticed, looking pleased with his threat.

"No one's going to find you out here."

The guys had to be looking for me by now, but as good as they were, how would they find me if this place was as remote as Daniel suggested? I looked out to the highway, which was inked in darkness, a dimly lit overhead sign showing each side of the road lined with thick foliage, and not a single streetlight. He whirled me around. "Hold still."

We were standing in the parking lot of a rundown motel, a few of the rooms faintly lit. There were at least a dozen junkers scattered about and one tricked-out truck.

Willing myself to remain calm, I concentrated on not stumbling as I hobbled across the gravel driveway, putting my weight on my one good shoe and expecting to fall on my face with every step. Daniel pushed me up a short set of wooden steps and jerked me to a stop. I grasped at the wooden railing, hissing as a splinter embedded itself in my palm. A door groaned on its hinges, and the smell that wafted out had an instant effect on my stomach. I turned and heaved over the railing.

"Just great. You got any more coming up, do it now, or you'll sit with it running down your front."

I hung my head and continued to be sick until there was nothing left in my stomach.

After a short reprieve, fingers dug back into my arm. I was propelled forward and tripped over the threshold, my head making contact with the wall. I slid to the floor inside the room, happy to be sitting on carpet, even though it felt sticky. I didn't dare risk sucking in another whiff of the stench that had wafted out when he opened the door. He jerked me up and shoved me into a chair, then took the cuffs off, yanking one wrist over and cuffing it to the arm of the chair. I bent forward and lifted the hem of my dress to cover my nose and suck in a couple of breaths.

The dingy motel room was furnished with the bare necessities—bed, dresser, two cheap chairs, and the small table where I sat. The only exit was the door we'd come through, since I assumed the only other door went to the bathroom. The one window was small, and even if I had the opportunity, I wasn't sure I could fit through it.

"Not quite what you're used to, now is it?" Daniel tossed a cloth briefcase on the table and flourished his hand around the four soulless walls. "You could've saved yourself all this drama if you'd just paid up. It's not like you can't afford it—my original asking price was pocket change for you. But you decided not to pay and now I've got a much better idea." He laughed with satisfaction. "Why settle for a single payment when I can get payments out of you for years to come? I need someone to support my lifestyle, and you certainly have the money."

I simply stared, not understanding what the heck he was talking about. Was he the one who'd attempted to extort Pryce? And how did he plan to milk us for continuous cash? I was pretty sure at this point that he'd kidnapped me for ransom, but no one continued to pay ransom after being released and he had nothing to hold over either me or Pryce. "I'm certain we can work something out," I said with more assurance than I felt.

"If you're thinking I killed Lili, I can assure you that I didn't. Why would I get rid of my meal ticket?" Daniel sneered. "All she had to do was marry that oaf and we'd have both been secure. But some woman sold her a pack of lies about Pryce losing all his money. I had a quick check run, which proved that the story she was fed was false, and I told her so. I wasn't one hundred percent certain, but nothing else made any sense—that woman was obviously a jealous shrew who wanted Pryce for herself."

My feet burned, and I edged off my shoes to rub feeling back into my toes.

"Put those back on. Now," Daniel ordered.

"You think you're going to make a run for it across the gravel? Good luck. If by some chance I can't catch you, which I doubt, I'm a good shot."

I shivered at the coldness of his voice and slid my toes back into my shoes.

"Lili and I did fight, and a lot. I was at that farce of a wedding, and when I found out she called it off, I admit I punched her, but I knew we could salvage the relationship since we had in the past. Then she blurted out that she was not only dumping Pryce but me. I might've killed her on the spot if she hadn't gotten out the door and into the rental car before I could grab her. My guess is that she went straight to the airport, which I didn't expect. I never saw her again— next thing I knew, she was reported dead. All I could think about was who's going to pay my bills now? Squeezing it out of your husband didn't work, so that left you, and here we are."

"Don't you have another wife?"

"Stupid woman. She had a job that she quit— it barely covered the bills, but it was something. Now she's only good for one thing, and I don't need her around all day for that, driving me nuts with her whining."

"What do you want? I'm certain we can come to an agreement." One that would include letting me go. Was he that stupid? I hoped he wouldn't factor in that I could identify him... and would in a heartbeat.

"You have no one to blame but yourself. All

you had to do was pay up." His eyes were unnaturally bright. "Instead, you set a trap. Look how that turned out. Now you're the one in the trap."

"I had nothing to do with your attempt to extort money from Pryce not going as planned." I breathed into the material of my skirt to keep calm.

"After the setup failed and I watched the kid get arrested, I followed the car to the police station and kept an eye out. When he was released after several hours, I knew he'd blabbed after he'd been explicitly told not to. Should have listened. Tracked him down and gave him a lesson in keeping his mouth shut. He won't be blabbing everything he knows in the future."

I grimaced, hoping that despite what he said, the kid was still alive. I wasn't sure whether I believed Daniel when he said he hadn't killed Lili.

"Got to thinking…" He tapped his temple, amused with himself. "Maybe Thornton did lose his fortune like he said, though I couldn't find evidence of that. But if he had…" He paused. "Perusing the gossip sheets, I figured out pretty quickly you're the real hot ticket. A little more investigation, and I found to my surprise and happiness that you could buy and sell him several times over."

"I—" Wanted to deny his suppositions, but why bother, since he'd know it was a lie?

Daniel sliced his finger across his neck in annoyance. "If you think I can't see through your lies, think again. So don't waste your breath. I don't think I'm wrong, but even if I am, your hub has plenty of cash and my guess is he'll pay to get you back. I've seen the way the man looks at you."

How? But I didn't ask. Apparently, he'd been lurking around—a lot—and we'd missed it. Not like we'd even been looking. We thought we were living in a safe place and had kept our personal information private.

"You need to work at covering your emotions. I can see everything you're thinking. I've been tracking you since you showed up at my place with that lame story. My first break came when I had a friend run your license number. It did take some work to figure out who was who, but it was worth every bit of frustration when I found out you were Rella Cabot, billionaire. How many of those do you meet? Then, to find out you were married to the murderer... Too bad, I'd have made a play for you myself. And might still have when he got shipped off to prison, but we know how that turned out."

I cringed internally and was certain it showed on my face. He glared.

"Before the charges were dropped, I entertained a variety of ways of getting you to marry me. Once I thought about it more, though, I realized that this is the better route. This way,

I've got total control over you—you'll do what I say when I say it."

"If money's what you're after, name a one-time lump sum, and we'll be done with it. Give me the account number, and I'll transfer the money." I struggled to keep my voice steady.

He sneered, quickly replaced by an unpleasant smile. "I'd say one million, but expenses add up. Adding a premium for giving up having you under my control would soothe me some."

"Five million and we're done here," I countered. "We each go our own way and never mention the other's name again."

"That and a first-class trip out of town. Lili's death will probably haunt me for a while, and I definitely don't want any fingers pointed my way. I've managed to stay off the police's radar and want it to stay that way."

I was surprised that being Lili's husband hadn't garnered him a visit. And then there was his bigamy... or maybe he only showed up as married to Amy Peters.

"Give me what I want, and you'll be free to go. I'll head out of town and leave you on a deserted stretch of highway, and you can go wherever you want from there. I know just the isolated spot to shove you out of the car."

I wanted to up the payoff to include shoes, but he'd probably laugh, knowing that bare feet would slow me down even more. Plus, since I wasn't sure where we were or what drop-off he had in mind, deserted could mean anything. "You do know that amount of money can't just be transferred with the touch of a button?" I said, trying to buy time. At his snort, I added, "It can be done, but I'll need a laptop and wi-fi." Though I wasn't sure this rathole had that amenity. Surely he'd done his homework; if not, what did he have planned?

"Don't even think about double-crossing me. You do, and you'll be my first kill. Next up, your hubby. All I'd have to do is load your bodies in the trunk, and dump them where they'd never be found, then sell the car for scrap." Daniel brushed his hands together.

My stomach twisted into another hard knot. Not wanting to think about what the disposal of two bodies would entail or how he was so sure they'd disappear forever, I squeezed my eyes tight and told the images to beat it. This was no time to be sick again, even if I had anything left in my stomach, although aiming for him would be satisfying.

"You know, I'm a thorough man... researching, spying," Daniel boasted. "After watching you in action, I instinctively knew that you wouldn't be a pushover. I crept around your property on several occasions—your residents aren't nearly as careful as you think they are— finally getting into the garage and then the lobby. Never did make it into the elevator. I wasn't ready to execute my plan tonight, but when opportunity knocks... I'd planned all along to bring you to this remote area, and knowing we'd need wi-fi, I checked before choosing this motel. Don't think you're going to screw me — neither of us will be going anywhere until I get confirmation that your deposit has cleared. Handy, huh?"

What was I supposed to say?

Chapter Twenty-Seven

Repulsed by the smug arrogance in his eyes, I knew to choose my words carefully going forward. "I'm ready to make the transfer." I hoped that soon after, I'd be free to leave. Part of me found it hard to believe he'd let me go. The other part hoped.

He unzipped his briefcase and pulled out a laptop that he set in front of me. He flipped up the lid and turned it on, then sat next to me and pulled out his phone. "Now get to work. And don't think I won't be monitoring your every click. I catch you doing anything except what you're told, and..." He laughed evilly.

"I need both hands." I rattled the cuffed one.

He reached in his bag and produced another pair of handcuffs, waving them in my face. "Can't have you running off." He bent down, cuffing one ankle to a chair leg before releasing my wrist. He pulled his chair closer to mine, practically sitting on top of me, with an unobstructed view of the screen.

Surprisingly, Daniel only paid about half-attention to what I was doing, busy scrolling through his phone instead, although he glanced over frequently. He didn't notice that I deliberately put in the wrong password twice, which would trigger an email to be sent for verification. "The bank software doesn't recognize this machine, so I have to jump through some hoops to get in," I said before he noticed and took a closer look. He appeared to buy my explanation, leaning in as I started the verification process.

After Avery's legal problems when an embezzler targeted one of her clients, she'd put an alert on all her clients' accounts, ensuring that anytime a transfer was made, an email would be sent to her. As soon as she saw I was transferring that much money, she'd know something was wrong—if she didn't already know I'd gone missing—and be all over it.

Daniel had set his phone down and was hanging his head over my shoulder, his breath hot on my cheek. I swallowed my shudders.

Under his watchful eye and without stalling, I answered the security questions and verified the account. "I'll need your bank information to make the transfer. You should know that I'll have to make transfers from several accounts, as no one account has enough to do it in one."

He grunted, reaching in his pocket and pulling out a sheet of paper, which he slapped down in front of me.

In order to buy time, I worked as slowly as possible. I wasn't convinced that Daniel would let me go, so I needed a plan of my own. This was where I needed Harper or Avery.

It didn't take long for Daniel to get restless. He got up, paced the room, looked out the window, opened the drawers and the closet, which was nothing more than an opening in the wall. Suddenly, he stomped across the room and yanked down the phone that hung on the wall next to the bed, throwing it on the floor. "Try anything, and you'll rot here." He took up watch at the window again.

My anxiety levels soared, even though he appeared to have lost interest in what I was doing on the computer. Maybe he thought he'd scared me into doing exactly what he wanted. Basically, he had. I could only hope that my intentional flubs had been enough to gain attention.

As Daniel grew more agitated and began pacing the room, I finally transferred the money. "It's done," I called out.

He sat on the edge of the bed, taking his phone out of his pocket and flicking his fingers across the screen. After several minutes of staring at the screen, he demanded, "How long does this take?"

"Minutes usually, but then, I've never transferred that much money before."

The minutes ticked by, and he alternated between pacing and glaring at his phone.

"If you've—" His phone dinged. He swiped

the screen, and his mouth curved up in a chilling grin.

Just then, the fire alarm went off. It was deafening.

He grabbed a scarf from his briefcase just as I unleashed an ear-piercing scream. He slapped me, wrapped the scarf around my mouth and jerked it tight, then grabbed his laptop and briefcase. "I'd been debating what I was going to do with you. But now… if you're lucky, you'll die of smoke inhalation before the flames reach you." With a final parting glance, he left.

Thankfully, he'd forgotten my hands weren't secured, and as soon as the door closed, I started working at the knot of the gag and got it off. I'd already checked out the room, but I did it again, hoping I'd missed an exit. But there was only the one. I had to get out the same way as Daniel, without him seeing me, though I doubted he'd stick around to watch the building burn down. I half-stood, struggling to balance on one leg, grabbed the back of the chair. I inched forward, tried to twist the chair sideways. That hurt, so I pulled it to my side. I managed to drag the chair, then stumbled and fell, the chair landing on top of me, wrenching my ankle in the process. I lay there, hissing at the pain. *Get moving,* I told myself. I edged toward the bed, one painful thump at a time. Now, how to get the chair back upright and me along with it? Luck was with me, and I managed to get it on its feet. Then, one hand on the back of the chair, I inched toward the door, set the chair off to the side, and slid onto the seat.

The alarm stopped. I expected to hear screams, but instead, there were several seconds of silence, and then the sound of the television coming from the next room. I hoped that meant I wouldn't be burning to death. No sirens in the distance, which I took as a good sign. Reaching for the handle, hoping not to see Daniel's face, I jerked open the door. It was pitch-dark outside, the only light coming from a handful of stars overhead. I could barely make out the cars in the parking lot; apparently, the fire alarm hadn't sent people scurrying. I eyed the walkway that ran the length of the one-story building with a set of four steps leading up to the doors in three different locations. Over the wood railing, I caught sight of a lit cigarette—a man was smoking, sitting on the top step at the far end. I could hear the voices of a couple men in the parking lot and see the silhouette of one sitting on the trunk of a car.

"Hey," I yelled, waving my hand and hoping either of the men would look my way. The smoker did, and I yelled again. "Would you call the cops?"

He stared. Never taking his eyes off me, he took one last puff of his cigarette, put it out under his shoe, and stuck the remnant in his pocket. Without a word, he went back inside his room and shut the door. The men in the parking lot turned my way, staring, then ran back to their room without another glance my way.

I sucked in a deep breath and started screaming, continuing until my throat burned.

Finally, the door of the room next door flew open with a bang, and a woman stuck her head out.

"Over here." I waved.

"A drunk." She shook her head in disgust.

"No, I'm not—"

"You shut the hell up or I'll do it for you," she yelled at me; then, to someone behind her: "This is the last time we stay in a flea hole. Better to sleep in the car."

"Please call the cops. Please."

"I'm minding my own business like everyone else here." She slammed the door.

Despite her warning, I screamed again, hoping someone else would hear.

The woman from next door threw the door open again and stepped outside, facing me. "I've had enough," she screamed shrilly. "I dare you to do it again." She clenched her fists.

I nodded meekly. It wouldn't have surprised me if the door came off the hinges from the force she used to close it. Moving the chair backward across the threshold proved more difficult than going forward, but I managed to inch my way back inside and got the door closed and locked. Chair in tow, I hobbled over to the end of the bed and chose the side closest to the window. Would

I be safe if Daniel came back? Probably not, but then, why would he? He got the cash he wanted. If I weren't cuffed to a chair, I would've pushed the dresser in front of the door. But if I could've done that, I'd be out of here already. The best I could hope for was maid service, and that she'd show up early. Wonder when check-out was? I leaned back, elevating my free leg on the chair seat.

I didn't know how much time passed before I heard something outside. The clock on the bedside table blinked incessantly; who knew how long it'd been since it last moved off twelve o'clock. It was still dark outside. I rubbed my wrist, where earlier there'd been handcuffs, and sat up, listening hard. There were definitely voices coming from outside. I leaned toward the window, my ankle reminding me to move slow, and jerked open the curtain to see red lights flashing in the parking lot. The window wouldn't open, and I didn't have anything to break the glass.

Someone was knocking on the door next to mine. That woman wasn't going to be happy.

A light flashed in my face. "Help," I yelled.

"Found her," someone yelled, followed by running footsteps.

I tried not to lose it when they shut off their flashlight, hoping they were here for me and wouldn't just leave.

More running footsteps. With a loud bang, the

door flew open, and a cop stood in the doorway, a scrawny dude trying to look over his shoulder. "Step back," the cop barked at him, then asked, "Rella Cabot?"

"Yes." I burst into tears.

Chapter Twenty-Eight

The cop checked me over, took out a key, and got the cuff off my ankle. Another cop showed up, and the two talked as paramedics entered the room with a gurney. They asked a few questions before loading me up and strapping me down. A third cop appeared at my side and had a couple more questions that I barely heard and answered inanely, as I was busy staring at Pryce, who'd grabbed my hand and brushed a quick kiss across my knuckles before I was rolled outside.

"I knew you'd find me." I leaned into his fingers, which trailed down my cheek before he was told to stand back.

As I was loaded into the back of an ambulance, all I could think was that the only thing that made going to the hospital tolerable was having Pryce by my side.

It was a short ride. I was rolled into the emergency entrance and checked over by a doctor, after which, he ordered a few tests. Once I was moved into a room to wait for the results of the tests, the last cop from the motel showed up to question me. I related everything that'd happened in detail, after which he had a few more questions. He wanted a formal sit-down at police headquarters later to get my statement in writing, and I assured him I'd be there.

Pryce, who was sitting across the room, looked ready to explode. After giving the cop our contact information, he followed him into the hall, and I suspect he had a few questions of his own.

The doctor came in with a smile and announced, "Your tests were all good—not a single issue. You're cleared to be released."

It was a new morning, and I'm still alive. The sun streamed through the windows, and I took a moment to appreciate it as I thought I might never see another day again.

It took a few hours and was after dawn before I was signed out and headed home. Pryce never left my side.

Once in the car, I reclined the seat, feeling sore all over, then grabbed Pryce's hand and held on tight. I never wanted to let go. "When we get home, after a long shower, I'll have shrimp tacos and a margarita. Or just make that a shot. A little lime."

"Not happening, babe." Noting my sigh, he added, "You're going to have to wait on the alcohol. But the tacos—done. When you're feeling one hundred percent, I'll make it up you—take you to a fun restaurant and we'll order a pitcher."

"Don't think I'll forget," I said with a strained

smile. "Maybe after a quick nap, I'll be up to talking to Avery. Tomorrow's soon enough to talk to her; we'll both be rested then."

"I'd hold them off if I could, but they pretty much do what they want." Pryce laughed. "They're both eager to see you. A little warning: Avery's spitting mad. She wanted to be at the motel when the cops found you."

My laughter sounded more like a gurgling noise. "I'm impressed that you were able to stop her."

"Not me." He shook his head with a grimace. "Seven. Rumor has it that it took muscle to keep her from being at your side. I texted him that you'd been sprung and we were on the way home so he could be the one to break the news, which should ensure that he'll get lucky again in this lifetime."

I laughed along with Pryce. "I'm not worried about those two. I'm very happy that she has someone who can temper her wilder impulses, and she still looks at him like he's tasty."

He pulled into the underground garage and parked.

For the first time, I didn't feel safe on my own property and didn't want to get out. I scanned the cars for one I didn't recognize, though it was hard, since I didn't know them all. Tightening security would be at the top of my list.

Pryce came around and opened my door, then leaned in, kissed me, and helped me out. "I promise not to let anything happen to you."

"I'm fine." I clutched harder at his arm. "Just weirded out by being attacked on my own property, which I'd thought was safe."

"Grey and Seven are in the process of reviewing all the security around here and will give you a report on everything they suggest. One thing they've already mentioned is installing cameras at all entrances, and that includes here in the garage." Pryce opened the door to the lobby area, and I looked around before stepping through. We got in the elevator, and he enveloped my hand in his as we rode up to the top floor. "Avery, your head of security, made it clear that she'll have a few suggestions of her own. I wouldn't have thought her qualified, but she disabused me of that notion. She's how we found out that you'd been kidnapped."

"Avery came to me one day and suggested the job title. To be truthful, I thought she was kidding. How long have I known her? I should've known better, especially after the way she took over management of Harper's dad's office building." I remembered the conversation fairly vaguely, having only been half-listening. "I'd give her a raise if she were getting paid. As it is, I'll have dozens of donuts delivered."

Pryce chuckled. "Apparently she's got a list of ideas and is excited to unveil all of them."

The elevator opened, and I was happy to see my front door, as I'd wondered a time or two if

I'd make it back here. "Later this morning, how about we go down to the beach? Sinking my toes in the sand would be good for me."

Pryce blocked the door, clearing his throat, a guilty look on his face. "You're going to need to put that thought on hold."

"It's a surprise, isn't it?" He nodded. I made a face. "I have the bestest of friends."

"I'm convinced there isn't anything they wouldn't do for you." Pryce unlocked the door. I was surprised by how quiet it was, even with Bruno by the door, eager to say hello. I scratched his head and looked around tentatively, braced for shouts and confetti.

Avery came bounding in from the balcony, Harper a step behind her. "I wanted to scream surprise, but the consensus was to keep it low-key." She made a face.

The two women ran over and enveloped me in a soft hug, and I started to cry.

"Oh no you don't." Avery wiped my eyes with the corner of her shirt. "That dickface isn't worth a single tear."

Reading my mind, they led me to my bedroom and, while I showered, picked out a comfortable colorful sundress for me to wear. Then led me outside and gently shoved me into a chair. Avery picked my feet up and put them on the footrest while Harper handed me an orange juice.

"I'm fine," I told them, waving to Grey and Seven. I eyed the juice, which looked good, but...

I turned to my friends and mimed drinking. "Could you sneak me something?" Okay, that might've come out louder than I intended.

"I saw that." Pryce pointed a stern finger at me.

Harper put her finger under my chin and turned my face from side to side. "You'll have a spectacular bruise for a while. When you're ready to go out, we'll go through Avery's sunglasses stash and find a pair that will cover most everything, and we'll have that drink."

I knew they wanted to hear firsthand about my ordeal with Daniel and would have a few follow-up questions of their own. But first, food. "Something smells really good." My stomach grumbled in agreement.

"The guys insisted on cooking. They claim they can cook." Avery wrinkled her nose, amusement on her face.

Pryce mouthed *sorry*. I gave a slight shake of my head, telegraphing, *This is just what I need – friends.* And later we'd have tacos. "It's lucky that we got here in time for Pryce to tell Grey and Seven what to do."

All three men laughed.

Pryce kissed the top of my head, staying close but ready to offer up a cooking tip or two. Seven tossed him an apron to match the ones the other two had donned over their shorts. Grey commandeered the grill, and the other two traded off jobs, going back and forth to the kitchen. The last trip, Pryce refilled all our glasses.

At that point, Harper, who'd disappeared, came back. "Got you something special," she said with a wink and set a tray on the side table next to me. "This concoction has been taste-tested by Avery and me, and it's not bad." Noting my skeptical look, she added, "Promise," and handed me a margarita glass.

I took a closer look, and it appeared to be the real deal but probably wasn't, since Pryce eyed the glass with a smirk instead of having a hissy fit. A girl could hope. I took a sip. "Not bad." I took another sip. "Except that you were stingy on the alcohol," I said to Harper and Avery, who were hovering.

"The non-alkie version," Harper said. "Once your guard gives his approval to sauce it up, we'll have a girls lunch at our favorite restaurant with pitchers all around. And I'll have a driver on standby to get us home."

Grey pointed at himself, volunteering for the job.

"If we choose the Ocean House, we need to sneak in something healthy to feed the birds," I said.

Avery groaned. "Management put a stop to that. Last week, when Seven and I were there for dinner, they caught another couple in the act and asked them to leave. The server told us they'd had signs made, warning customers that if they were caught feeding the birds, they'd be tossed. Apparently it's too messy and some of the customers complain."

"Breakfast is ready," Grey announced. "We decided to see if I could replicate one of your favorites on the grill." He slid a frittata out of a large frying pan onto a platter.

We all took seats at the table. The biggest selling point of this building was the view of the waters of Biscayne Bay below, and it never got old.

Grey set down another platter of hash browns. Seven and Pryce brought fresh fruit and muffins that were still warm from the oven. Lots of choices, and it all looked good.

It smelled delicious. Despite all my stomach's grumbling about being hungry, I could only hope that I could do this meal justice and not just pick.

It was fun to sit and listen to the guys kid one another.

I knew they had questions, probably a few more than I did, but they were giving me a chance to relax. By the end of the meal, my eyes were drooping. I tried to fight the fatigue and lost, my head coming to rest on Pryce's shoulder, my eyes closed. I was vaguely aware of him helping me to my feet and into the house. When he laid me down on the bed, I was out.

Chapter Twenty-Nine

I'd been hiding out the last couple of days, feigning sleep and keeping a book under my pillow to keep from slipping into boredom. The pain in my bruised and battered body went down considerably after a day, and I stopped taking Tylenol, which only made me sleepy. I wanted to be on full alert and aware of everything going on around me. How dare Daniel scare me in my own home? I refused to think about going down to the garage by myself for the first time. How many trips would it take to get over the fear?

The police had requested my presence today, which meant I had to get up and get dressed. When I first got the call, Pryce got hot on the phone and arranged for Cruz to meet us there.

We met Cruz at police headquarters, and after we cleared security, he ushered us up to the second floor. The woman at the desk pointed us down the hall, and Pryce had to take a seat in the waiting area. "Not happy" didn't quite cover the militant look on his face. Cruz and I entered the conference room, where two detectives sat laughing. That stopped once we crossed the threshold.

"Tell us what happened," one of them said, getting right to the point after announcing that everything would be taped.

I went over the events of that dreadful day, not once, but twice. And there were more questions, to which I gave straightforward answers. Cruz patted my arm a couple of times, and I knew that was his way of approving of my following his advice. As we rode up in the elevator, he'd admonished, "Give truthful, direct responses. Don't wade off into the weeds."

Finally, they thanked me for coming, and one of the detectives stood and walked out.

"I have a question," I said before the other detective ran out of the room. "Has Daniel Stone been arrested yet?" I'd searched the internet but hadn't found a word about him or his crimes.

"We can't discuss the case. The district attorney's office will be in touch," he said, then stood, waiting for us to do the same.

Why did that sound like a complete brush-off? Weren't victims kept updated? "When will that be?" I knew I sounded snarkier than I meant to.

"Mr. Campion can keep you updated."

Cruz squeezed my arm, which I assumed was a silent... what? *Don't ask questions?* "I've got it covered," he assured me, "and will get you an update today."

I reluctantly stood, thinking Cruz was behind

me, but when I turned at the door, he was in conversation with the detective. I continued to the reception area and filled Pryce in.

"We'll give Cruz five minutes. If he's a no-show, we're leaving," Pryce grumped.

Cruz cut it close, strolling out with a minute to spare and walking over to us. "No charges have been filed against Daniel Stone, as the case is still under investigation. I've got a connection in the DA's office and will give him a call. The second the arrest happens, I'll let you know." He promised to keep in touch, and we left the building, going in different directions.

It was a quick trek back to the car. Pryce held the door, and I got in and leaned back against the seat, closing my eyes. "I don't think the detectives believed me." Daniel—extorter, kidnapper, maybe murderer—was on the loose, and that made me nauseous. He had to know that the money transfers had been reversed. Wouldn't that make him crazy to get even and ensure I didn't walk away unscathed?

Pryce slid into the driver's seat and pulled out his phone, which was ringing. "Hello yourself," he barked, then drew a breath to calm down and relayed a shortened version of the meeting. "You and Seven are the ones with cop connections. Find out what's going on with this case. Why hasn't Daniel Stone been arrested? Last I heard, none of what he did was remotely legal." Whatever questions Grey threw at him, his answers were clipped. "We're on our way home." He turned to me for confirmation, and I nodded.

"I want a meeting," I said.

He relayed that. "See you in a few."

* * *

Not sure if it was a coin flip or what, but the meeting was being held on Avery's balcony. Our outside spaces mirrored each other, and we all shared the same view. Any excuse to sit outside was a philosophy that had bonded us long ago. The drink choices were iced tea, water, and beer. If you wanted the latter, you helped yourself from the outside refrigerator.

Grey appeared ready to take control of the meeting, but before he could start talking, my frustration got the better of me. "Daniel is still out there lurking around. He hasn't been arrested. There isn't even a warrant out for his arrest!" I stopped short of snapping. "The frustration on your face makes me have to ask: is he even under investigation, and if not, why not?"

An uncomfortable tension settled over the table.

"It's my understanding that the cops have questioned Daniel. What came of that?" Pryce asked. "Like you, I want to see him rotting behind bars. Until that happens, I'm not letting you out of my sight."

"How could Daniel possibly be roaming free?"

"I was about to tell you that my source couldn't provide any information since he's part of the investigation," Grey said, looking to Seven to take over.

I was embarrassed at having cut him off.

"Daniel has an alibi—two of them, in fact," Seven said. "On the surface, this case looks like a 'he said, she said.' The cops are leaning on the witnesses, since they didn't find them particularly believable and found your attention to detail far more credible."

"Daniel told the cops that you were stalking him, wouldn't take no for an answer, and when you ran out of options, you resorted to making stuff up," Avery said.

"What a load of…" I sputtered.

"We're going to treat you like one of our clients," Grey said. "Do you mind going over everything from the beginning?"

"Ask me anything; I want to be as helpful as I can." I relayed everything that happened that day, from when I stepped into the lobby until the cops rescued me.

"Interesting that Daniel claimed not to have killed Lili. He's at the top of the list of people I'd want to talk to if I were in charge of the case," Grey said.

"He was adamant that he didn't kill her. Did I believe him? Not particularly. He told me the only reason I wasn't dead was because he wasn't a killer. But at the time, the money hadn't been transferred yet. Who knows what he'd have done after if the fire alarm hadn't gone off. Though he did leave me in the motel room thinking I'd burn to death." I shuddered.

"Found out that the building is notorious for false alarms," Grey said.

"Fire department needs to stick a boot up their…" Pryce said in disgust.

"After the alarm went off and the place didn't go up in flames, I made my way over to the door and yelled for help. The woman in the next room couldn't've cared less; in fact, she threatened to shut me up." I squeezed my eyes closed, not wanting to remember. "I don't know how you found me; all I care is that you did and I got out in one piece."

"I was keeping an eye out for you after you called to say you were on your way home. I wanted to surprise you the minute you got here," Pryce said. "I know how long the drive takes, so I knew you were late. I hadn't started to worry yet, but I had started wondering where you were. Was about to call you when the intercom buzzed. It was a neighbor calling from the lobby, and she had your purse and briefcase. I went down to meet and thank her, then checked the garage, and our cars were all parked in their respective spaces. Still thinking there was a simple answer, though nothing I could come up with made any sense, I raced back upstairs, straight to Grey and Harper's place, and barely restrained myself from kicking in the door." He smiled at Harper. "Hearing what had me rattled, Harper promised that she wouldn't commit bodily harm for any damage."

"You're so nervy." I winked.

"You complain about us, and there you were, shouting your head off," Avery said, seeming impressed by the scene he'd made. "I barely got in the door before it closed in my face." She held out her thumb and forefinger—a scintilla of an inch was all the room she'd had. "Got the gist of what was happening and ran back home, grabbed my laptop, and yelled for Seven."

"Then you pulled up the security footage." Harper turned to Avery. "So glad you had Rella install all those cameras."

"Next time you want a lofty title, it's yours," I said.

The rest of us laughed. The changes Avery had made at the office building had all been for the better.

Avery smiled, but it disappeared fast. "It didn't take me long to review the footage, and I watched as you were dragged to a car. Daniel was good at hiding his face, as there wasn't a clear shot of him, but I did get the license plate number."

"Even though it turned out to be stolen, it was still useful information," Seven assured her.

"The cops recovered it yesterday, and it's being dusted for prints," Grey informed us.

"It really surprises me that he just dumped the car," I said. "Daniel boasted that he could make it disappear, along with mine and Pryce's bodies, if he caught Pryce interfering in his scheme or anything went wrong with the money transfer."

"Once Avery showed us the footage, I called a couple of my friends on the local force and they came over and watched it. They put out an immediate APB on you," Seven said. "Those same friends haven't been assigned to the case but are able to stay on top of any new information."

"As you know, I put alerts on all my clients' accounts to track any activity out of the norm," Avery said, "but I didn't think to check your accounts until I got an alert about a failed login. No way it could be a coincidence."

"I counted on you having some kind of wizardry in place that would alert you when I deliberately muffed the password. It also bought me some time."

"At first, I thought it was a hacker. Then came a notification of two large transfers, and that was enough of a red flag that I knew something bad had happened. But what? Then the money went into the account of a person I'd never heard of. I gave the transaction time to clear and be verified, then snatched it back. Not knowing how savvy the person was, I wasn't going to wait and risk chasing it all over the country or the world."

"That's how we got a location on you," Grey said. "Avery tracked the IP address before the computer was shut down and figured we hit pay dirt when it turned out to be a remote area. A search showed only a gas station and a fleabag motel out there."

"Called that in immediately," Seven said. "Rattled my nerves when I turned over the location to my cop friend and he laughed, and not in a good way. Told me that more than one person had died on the property, usually a drug overdose. The property's a big thorn in the side of law enforcement, and they'd love to shut it down. The owner claims ignorance of all the illegal activities that go on, alleging innocence as he's never on site. They've about compiled enough evidence to get an order to put the man out of business. So they were happy to go shine their lights in the windows."

"Once we figured out that the motel was where you were being held, we shot out of here," Grey said. "Pryce was ahead of us all, and no amount of shouting to hold up, that one of us would go with him, slowed him down. We weren't far behind, despite his lead."

"My chat with the desk guy at the motel yielded useful information." Seven flexed his muscles.

"Is that what you call it when you drag the guy over the counter by his dirty t-shirt?" Grey smirked at him.

"He had a major 'tude about being woken up in the middle of the night. All it took was the threat of a punch or two, and he started answering questions."

"I offered a bribe first, but he whined that no amount of money was worth what the owner of the building would do to him if he found out he'd told anyone anything," Grey said. "Apparently the owner has ears everywhere. The desk guy shuddered and said, 'There won't be enough body parts to identify me.' He only changed his tune after Seven threatened to beat him. Dude finally talked, then Seven went soft and paid him anyway."

"Daniel must have been disappointed when he heard the place didn't burn down," I said, hoping images of that place didn't haunt me. "He had to know that I'd call the cops despite promising otherwise. He must have arranged that bogus alibi in advance."

"After you were hauled off in the ambulance, we stuck around," Grey said. "Knowing what we did of your statement, Seven called Avery and got Daniel's address for the cops. By that time, they'd gotten a report that the car we had on our security footage had been stolen. They headed over to Daniel's place, not expecting to find him home, and there he sat with his two alibis. Both women."

"Now what?" I asked. *Wait until he comes after me again?*

"You keep a low profile," Pryce said.

"That's a good idea, and it's easy for me to work from home," I said. "But maybe I should have WD arrange security for all of us. I'm not talking freebie either—send me the bill."

"Throw some hours to the guys who're always clamoring for more," Harper suggested to Grey.

"A guard or two on the property would be good to make sure that no one shifty shows up," Avery said. "When one of us wants to go somewhere, we snag a guard."

"That's a great idea." I dared Grey to say otherwise, but he nodded.

"I like the idea... a lot." Pryce side-hugged me.

Chapter Thirty

It had taken a day to set up, and now we had bodyguards stationed at the condos. Pryce and I planned to stay under the radar and work from home, our only exception running on the beach.

Both of us were early risers, and we were sitting at the island drinking coffee when my phone dinged with a text. "From Floyd James," I said and read the text aloud: *Be there within the hour.* When the subject of bodyguards came up, I'd been the first one to call dibs on everyone's favorite, Floyd, to bodyguard Pryce and me.

"This Floyd fellow even looks at you in an unprofessional way, I'll beat the heck out of him." Pryce air-boxed.

Conjuring up an image of how the knock-out would go down, I burst out laughing, tried to pull myself together, and only laughed harder.

"What?" He slapped his hand on the counter. "You don't think I can protect what's mine?"

"Hon…" I leaned forward and brushed his lips with mine. "Super swear, there's no one else for me. At least, not right now." I winked.

Pryce hopped off his stool and came around the island in a flash, grabbing me and silencing my squeals with a kiss.

There was a knock on the door, not quite a pounding, but it could be heard throughout the unit. We had a few choices for who it could be, but my bet was Floyd. Good thing we were already dressed, since time flies when you're making out in the kitchen.

Pryce crossed the room and opened the door, with me right on his heels.

An enormous man strode in. He was reminiscent of a battle tank and stood ramrod straight in a pair of well-fitting jeans and a crisp dress shirt, his brown hair tightly cropped. His cold brown eyes lit on me and softened. He winked. "Mrs. Thornton."

I stepped around Pryce and introduced the two men. Although Pryce was well over six feet, Floyd had several inches on him.

"I just told my wife that if you made a pass at her, I'd beat you up, and I can see why she laughed," Pryce told the man.

Floyd laughed as he crossed over to the hutch and set down his briefcase, casually checking out the rooms he could see. "There are way too many women to share my charms with to go poaching and end up getting this pretty face rearranged." He turned to me. "Mom sends her best."

"I just talked to her yesterday and told her I snatched up your services before anyone else could lay claim. She told me, 'Smart move.'" I motioned for the guys to follow me to the kitchen. "I'm assuming that Avery got you fixed up with security cards."

"That Avery is one organized chick. You don't have to ask a dozen times—once and it's done." Floyd slid onto a stool.

"Coffee?" I asked, and he nodded. I got a mug, filled it from the pot Pryce had made, and set a fresh cup in front of Pryce while I was at it. "Any time you want something cold to drink, or anything else, help yourself." I pointed to the refrigerator.

"I know you've been briefed on what's going on," Pryce said. "Wish I could say that I had new information, but no such luck. Guarding the two of us might be boring, as Rella and I have agreed to stick close to home, with the exception of the beach, until Daniel's arrested."

"But it's good to know that should we need to go out, we have someone covering our backs." I didn't know when I'd stop being afraid to leave the house.

"During downtimes, I've got paperwork in my briefcase that needs attention," Floyd said. "When we venture out, I can hang back and follow you two or be right by your side. I recommend changing it up every time. But however you want to handle it is fine with me."

"Rella's first priority. Whether she's here or needs to go into the office, I want you right by her side," Pryce said adamantly. "Daniel Stone has shown himself to be adept at getting past security measures."

"I know that taking a 'wait and see what happens' stance is hard on the nerves," Floyd said. "The other option is to go places in the hopes of drawing him out and see if he makes a move. If he were to show up anywhere, you'd know he's got eyes on you and we have to tighten up security."

The sitting duck idea made me queasy, and I knew from the way Pryce grabbed my hand, holding it in a tight squeeze, that he agreed with me.

Floyd's phone rang. He got up to answer it and moved several feet away, barked a few responses, then hung up. "That wasn't good news. Trace was out last night and got mugged. A car clipped him crossing the street, and he ended up in the gutter. The driver got out, his face covered with a mask, stole his wallet and phone, and sped off."

Trace was a young guy who'd helped Avery and Seven out in the past. When Avery found out that he and his brother lived in a storage room, she asked me for help. I found them what was supposed to be a temporary situation, but Floyd's mother, Rosa, took them in as her own and didn't want to hear about them moving. It'd turned out to be good for both her and the boys.

"Is he in the hospital?" I asked with a worried sigh. "Avery's going to want to know."

"By the time the cops arrived, he'd managed

to pick himself up out of the street. After answering their questions, he turned down their offer to call an ambulance. It took him a while to get back on his motorcycle and get home… but just barely because the bike's acting wonky. He borrowed his brother's phone to call me. He's hiding out in his bedroom, waiting for Mom to leave so he doesn't have to tell her what happened. And when she finds out…" Floyd laughed humorlessly. "Once she's done hovering and making sure he's back on his feet, she'll kill him."

"He was on his own so long, looking out for his brother—he just needs to be reminded that he has family now that has his back," I said.

"I told him I had someone who would look at the bike and wouldn't screw him on price. As for Mom, if he knows what's good for him, he'll get downstairs and tell her what happened," Floyd grumped, then took out his phone and made a call. "I'm here at Rella's. You mind if I put the call on speaker?" The answer must've been yes, as he hit a button.

"Just so you know, I did the same thing so Avery won't kill me." Seven laughed. "Afraid to ask what's up."

Floyd filled them in on what'd happened to Trace.

"I'll get someone over from the office to fill in for him on guard duty today. It's not a rush, since Avery's working from home," Seven said.

"I'll call to check on him. I'll also find out what he had in his wallet that needs to be cancelled and do it for him, since it would take him a lot longer than me," Avery volunteered. "As soon as I hang up, I'll wipe his phone of any information."

"While you've got him on the phone, insist that he take it easy for a day or two," Floyd said. "Instead of thinking he's invincible, he might listen to good advice."

"Don't worry, I'll threaten to nag the heck out of him if I hear of him doing otherwise." Avery laughed. "His biggest obstacle is going to be Mama Rosa; she's no pushover."

Anyone who knew the woman knew it was true.

After everyone agreed to stay in touch, we hung up.

"Carjackings are on the rise; not sure about motorcycles," Pryce said. "Trace's lucky he was able to walk away."

"We need a distraction. I vote for a run on the beach before it gets sweltering."

The three of us quickly changed and rode down in the elevator. When it was just me and Pryce, we'd walk along the shoreline; I would kick water on him, and he'd chase me for payback. However, adding Floyd to the equation resulted in the highly competitive men squaring off and challenging each other to a run. As they shot off, the thought of trying to keep up made me laugh. Instead, I brought up the rear, kicking sand every which way.

Eventually, the guys stopped and motioned for me to catch up. I laughed and shook my head. Based on their body language, they threw more challenges at one another before breaking into another run. They were definitely having a good time.

I walked in the low tide, enjoying the view of the Atlantic. This end of the beach was always quiet. Today, a handful of people had dragged their chairs out to the sand. A man played with his children in the water. I'd never paid attention before but suspected most users were local, as you had to know your way around to access the beach. Parking was also at a premium and required a hike.

Pryce and Floyd had upped their gamesmanship and were now shoving each other out of the lead. All the men who worked for WD were a good fit and had become fast friends. Though younger, even Trace fit in. I hoped he'd be back on the job soon, as it would be fun having him around.

I glanced up in time to see someone come out of the water and run up behind Floyd, who went down on his knees. The attacker kept moving, advancing on Pryce and hitting him with a long object. He landed face down on the sand, water lapping his face.

I broke into a run, screaming "help" over and

over, but we'd reached an isolated section of the beach, and my screams didn't garner any attention.

The attacker stepped on Pryce's head, smashing his face into the sand. There was a shout from Floyd, who'd made it back to his feet, and the person took off like a shot.

I ran up to Pryce, dropped down, and jerked his face out of the water, cradling it in my lap. He wasn't moving.

Floyd dropped to his knees and listened to Pryce's chest and checked his pulse. "He's breathing, so that's good." He took out his phone and called 911 to demand an ambulance.

"You okay?" I asked when he hung up.

"Feels like I was hit with a steel pipe." Floyd stood and stared around at the shoreline, then stalked over to where a pipe lay in the shallow water and took a couple of pictures. "Let's hope the cops are able to pull prints and can match them to someone. Don't touch it. You get a look at our attacker?" He surveyed the beach, looking ready to run after someone despite grimacing and rubbing his lower back. "Where the hell did they go?"

"Skinny pants and a hoodie came out of the water. I didn't notice them until they ran up behind you and you were on your knees. You need to sit." I pointed to the sand. "Take a few breaths of your own. Even though you've got a hard head, you need to be checked out."

"Disappeared awfully fast," Floyd grumbled.

"My focus was on Pryce, but I did see them shoot up the beach. My guess is they're familiar with the area and how to get out to the street."

A lifeguard came roaring down the beach on a four-wheeler, jumped out, and checked Pryce over, Floyd answering all his questions. A pickup truck made its way over the sand, and two more lifeguards hopped out and loaded Pryce into the back. They allowed me to ride along, and before I climbed in alongside Pryce, I insisted that Floyd be checked over.

"I'll take care of everything here," he assured me.

Pryce had his eyes open by the time we got out to the street, which was a great relief. An ambulance met us there and took us the rest of the way to the hospital.

Chapter Thirty-One

Pryce was taken into Emergency and admitted to a room. So I wouldn't be asked to leave, I quietly took a seat in the corner and watched, eagle-eyed, as the doctor checked him over, then had him wheeled away for tests. Having been through all this only a couple of days ago, I knew it was a fairly easy process. I called our friends, who'd already talked to Floyd, and requested a change of clothing.

It didn't take long for Harper, Avery, their guard—who I recognized but couldn't remember the name of—and Floyd to show up, two cops coming through the door immediately after them.

The cops pulled me aside and had more than a few questions, which I answered directly, remembering Cruz's advice. One question caught me off guard: "Did Mr. Thornton have any enemies?"

I told them about the murder case and the charges being dropped. His name didn't appear to ring a bell with them, and they looked surprised at my recitation of events. Finally, they took my information and gave me a card, then disappeared down the hall.

Floyd excused himself to get an update from the nurse's desk. By claiming to be Pryce's brother, he found out that when he was out of the MRI, he'd either be released or assigned a room upstairs. While they completed his MRI, I went into the bathroom and quickly changed clothes, then joined the other three in the room that Pryce wouldn't be coming back to.

"Have you been checked out?" I asked Floyd.

"No, he hasn't," Avery answered for him, then got up and left the room.

From the window, I could see her marching over to the nurse's desk.

"What's she doing?" Floyd grouched.

"You either do what you're told or I'm calling Mama Rosa. Your choice," I said.

Floyd laughed. "That's a good threat, even for a big guy like me. That little wisp of a woman could easily take me down."

Avery came back into the room with a nurse, who hurriedly checked something on the computer before turning to Floyd and motioning him to move to a chair closer to her.

"If he gives you any problems, let me know, and I'll call his mother," I said. Floyd groaned.

The nurse smiled, looking more than happy to be examining him. "If you'll wait outside?"

"Don't go anywhere without me," Floyd said in a stern tone.

"I'll be waiting." On my way out, the nurse

began asking questions.

Harper and Avery had already gone to the waiting room with their guard, and I joined them.

"Floyd was hit in the back, across the kidneys, and I'm happy he's being checked over. If I hadn't blackmailed him, he wouldn't have bothered." I sat down next to my friends.

"Knowing how we all like walking on the beach, I checked out the crime stats for the area ages ago. Not one incident," Avery said, "though the lifeguards have saved a couple of people from drowning."

I sat down next to my friends, and the three of us talked. It took a while before my phone pinged with a text from Floyd: *The coast is clear.* "I'm going to go and walk Floyd through the release process, then go find Pryce. Thank you for holding my hand."

We three-way hugged, and Harper and Avery left with their guard, but not before admonishing me to call as soon as Pryce was released.

Floyd gave me a wary smile as I walked back into the room. "Seriously, was that necessary?"

"Yes. Now what did she say?" I asked, sitting in a chair.

"Bonnet took my vitals. Turns out I'm strong as a horse." Floyd grinned.

"Did you happen to get *Bonnet's* phone number?"

He snorted. "Had to wait for a doctor to find

out that I have bruising around my kidney area, as if I didn't already know. Probably why it hurts like the devil."

"Since you had to strip for the doctor and you're dressed now, I take it that you're being released?"

"I can't believe I was caught totally off guard." Floyd sounded disgusted.

"You were down for like a nanosecond after someone clubbed you with a steel pipe, and in the kidneys no less." I grimaced. "Getting back on your feet is what sent the attacker on the run, certainly not my pitiful screams."

"You ran the description by me once already, but would you do it again?" Floyd asked.

"Slight build, covered from head to toe despite the weather. Impossible to tell if it was a man or woman. And hard to believe it was random."

"So much for thinking we were safe horsing around on the beach. Won't happen again," Floyd barked.

The doctor came back to tell me that, despite having a sizeable lump on the back of his head, Pryce was going to be fine. That said, he'd been transferred to a room for overnight observation, and if all went well, he'd be released in the morning. After that, he needed to rest and see his doctor for a follow-up appointment.

Floyd and I got the room number and maneuvered the halls, riding the elevator to the fourth floor.

"I'm going to be staying the night," I told him. "You don't have to hold my hand, since I won't be going anywhere. I can call you in the morning."

"Not happening. The rooms here have two couches; we can flip to see who gets which one." Floyd mimed a coin toss. He was still dressed in the same shorts and shirt that he was wearing on the beach.

"I thought you might like a shower and a change of clothes. Or not. I'm not trying to get rid of you, but I'll feel guilty about you having to hold my hand all night."

"Good idea." Floyd nodded. "I'll go home for a shower and change if you promise not to set foot out of the room until I get back."

"If you want to be my favorite person of all time, bring me back a couple of tacos with a side of guac, and sneak me in a margarita disguised as a soda."

Floyd laughed, shaking his head, which I took as a no to the drink.

We easily found the room, where Pryce was in bed, propped up and asleep, the machinery he was hooked up to showing that all was normal.

We'd stopped at the vending machine on the way, and I'd gotten a couple of waters and bag of mini cookies. I pulled up a chair next to the bed and sat, waving *see you later* to Floyd. He left, and I laid my head on the mattress. The television was on. I flipped around and found the sports channel, then closed my eyes.

* * *

Pryce slept the entire time Floyd was gone, opening his eyes several times, then going right back to sleep. However, at the smell of food, he woke up again, and I shared my tacos with him. He had a handful of questions for Floyd before he went back to sleep. I sacked out on one of the couches, and Floyd claimed a chair, which he positioned next to the door.

The doctor took his sweet time making the rounds the next morning, but when he finally arrived, he was happy with Pryce's progress and released him. Pryce didn't complain about the pain, but he winced often enough that I knew it was a problem.

Floyd helped me and Pryce into the back seat of his truck and drove us home, where he ordered us to stay put until he checked out all the corners of the garage before whistling that the coast was clear.

"When you're up to exercising again, I say we stick to the gym and pass on walking on the beach," I said on the way up in the elevator. "Not as much fun, but it does have a view. Lunch is at our place—I wanted to beg off, but when Harper said she'd bring pizza and a salad, I caved."

Floyd opened the door and preceded us inside, coming to an abrupt stop, his head turning from side to side. He turned back with a smirk. "I'd say your guests are all here. It's safe to come in, since I recognize all the faces."

Most of our friends and bodyguards were seated in the living room, where the sliders were open, some standing in the doorway of the balcony. Everyone clapped and hooted, waving wildly.

"Back in five." Pryce held up his fingers. "Then I want a drink," he said to me.

"No drink for you, and before you complain, those were your rules when I was released from the hospital," I said as I walked with him to the bedroom. "Do you need your back washed?"

"Not if I want to be back in five minutes." He went into the bathroom, and I laid out shorts and a shirt for him, then went back to the living room.

Chapter Thirty-Two

It was a week later when Grey called, saying he had news and that Pryce and I should come down the hall, where cold drinks were being served.

"If it was good news, wouldn't Grey just blurt it out?" I asked Pryce after I hung up.

"If those drinks have alcohol in them, that means the news could go either way." Pryce stood and pulled me to my feet.

We were the last to arrive. The rest had claimed seats in the living room as storm clouds rolled in, flashes of lightning streaking across the sky. I joined Harper and Avery and accepted a glass of iced tea.

"My friend on the force called," Seven said. "The case is still open, but there's not enough evidence to arrest Daniel. He's got his two alibi witnesses, who were thoroughly questioned with their lawyers present and didn't deviate from their story that they were with him that night, all night. The woman you mentioned from the motel left when the cops arrived, and the few guests who stuck around claimed not to have heard or seen anything."

"So what then?" I asked in an exasperated tone. "I bruised my face and handcuffed myself to a chair in a dive motel for the fun of it?"

"They do know you were grabbed, but there wasn't a clear shot of your attacker's face. Daniel told the police that you started stalking him after Pryce's arrest. He had a witness, one of the women, who said that you showed up at the condo looking for him and wouldn't say why," Grey told us.

"Did you go back by yourself?" Avery asked. I shook my head. "So Daniel's a bald-faced liar, which we already knew. When he said I could go look in the other room for the book I supposedly loaned Lili, I took the opportunity to check the rest of the rooms, and there was definitely no one else there. It was a two-bedroom unit, not large enough for anyone to hide in."

"My word against his. He painted me as unstable, and I unwittingly helped." I blew out a huff of frustration, and my hand sought Pryce's.

"You're telling us that Daniel's free to kidnap Rella again?" Pryce demanded. "You absolutely cannot go anywhere by yourself."

I nodded. "What about my friends? Are we all in danger?"

"Daniel's dangerous and crafty. So we all have to be aware of everything going on around us," Grey said.

"I got the distinct impression from Daniel's ramblings that he was hard up for money. How desperate is it going to make him that Avery took back every dime?" I remembered in vivid detail his threats to get even if things didn't go his way. He didn't get his money and I didn't die—no way he wasn't out for revenge.

"We've all got bodyguards. They're WD's best, and once they hear this news, they'll tighten security," Harper said after a silent exchange with Grey.

"My friend assured me that the case hasn't been closed," Seven said.

"Did you know that Grey and Seven went back to the motel to question the desk guy again and talk to a couple of the guests, and they didn't take me?" Avery pouted.

"That little visit didn't go anywhere." Grey half-laughed. "We weren't expecting to be met by a couple of thugs who'd been hired as security guards in light of recent problems. They were looking for an excuse to unleash an ass-kicking. Having been down that road before, we knew chances were good it would end in gunfire if we didn't back off, which we did."

"We assured them that we weren't looking for trouble, and when we turned to leave, one yelled "sissies" and laughed." Seven cracked his knuckles. "Grey's reminder that jail wasn't all that fun kept me moving forward."

"Speaking of that grungy motel, didn't they have security cameras?" Pryce asked.

"Several strategically placed around the

property, and not a single one of them worked; in fact, they never have. The owner said he just hadn't gotten around to hooking them up," Seven said with an eyeroll. "That's part of the service when they're installed, so he had to ask for them not to be connected. Or have them disconnected afterward."

I was about to ask *Now what?* for the umpteenth time when my phone rang, which I intended to ignore. However, Harper motioned for me to answer. I took it out of my pocket and checked the screen. "Cruzer," I announced. "Guess I should find out what he wants; might be important." I answered, "Good afternoon, Mr. Campion," expecting it to be his assistant, and was surprised when his voice rumbled over the line.

"The police would like to interview you again, as they have a few questions. I'll meet you at the station in two hours."

I shook my head. Was this where they believed Daniel and arrested me for filing a false report and wasting police resources? I must have agreed, however, because Cruz said, "See you there," and hung up. I quickly repeated the conversation to the room.

Pryce patted my hand. "I'll go with you."

Grey and Seven stared as though trying to read between the lines and figure out why the cops had more questions.

"What do you suppose this sit-down is all

about?" Pryce demanded.

"Good question. I'm going to find out." Seven took his phone out and made a call. Based on the questions, it was clear he was talking to his cop friend. "Thanks." He hung up. "He's going to ask around, see what he can find out, and get back to me. It'll take him a while."

"I have nothing to hide, and that includes my visit to Daniel. If asked, I'll tell the truth—I wanted to know more about Lili," I said.

"You run that by Cruz first," Grey admonished.

"He mentioned that we'd be meeting a few minutes early like before, I'm assuming to go over how to respond to questions. Trust me, I haven't forgotten those instructions." I finished off my iced tea, in need of the caffeine boost. "I need to change clothes." I stood, Pryce along with me.

"I'll keep you updated," he said to our friends, slinging his arm around me as we left.

I tried to ignore the concerned looks on their faces.

Chapter Thirty-Three

Pryce and I arrived at the station early, and Cruz was waiting for us. He motioned us over to a couple of empty chairs.

"Do you know what this meeting is about?" Pryce demanded once we sat down.

"They have more questions about Rella's kidnapping," Cruz told us.

"I'm not sure why they're bothering, since it appears they think I kidnapped myself."

"I believe you, and not just because you're my client." Cruz gave me a reassuring smile. "Only answer the questions put to you, and keep the answers short and direct."

The receptionist called him over, and he motioned for us to follow. We went upstairs, and once again, Pryce had to wait outside. After a quick kiss, I scurried after Cruz. The room was different, but the same two detectives waited for us.

"Start from the beginning," one directed.

Once again, I went over everything that happened that day, starting from when I stepped into the lobby. Although the interview was taped, both men made a couple of notes.

"The account the money was transferred to… the transaction was reversed not long after it was made. You said that Stone verified receiving payment and then left the motel room. How is that you ended up getting the money back?"

"My accounts are monitored for any unusual activity, and when the transfers happened, an alert was sent to my financial advisor, who—not recognizing the name as someone I'd done business with and not able to verify the transfer with me—reversed the transaction." I noticed their disbelieving looks.

"The account belongs to a George Dunner. What do you know about him?"

"Never heard of him," I said.

"Said the same thing about you, and we haven't found any connection. So far."

Daniel had been very good at covering his tracks and making it look as though I'd made everything up. He must be fuming at not being able to get his hands on the money.

"About your relationship with Liliana Ford…" Cop Two finally spoke up.

What? "I didn't know the woman. My only interest was in who really killed her, since at the time, Pryce Thornton had been charged, and I knew he was innocent."

"Where were you on the night of her death?"

"I never met her and didn't learn of her death until Pryce was arrested." I took note of Cruz's fingers tapping and took that to mean, 'Shorter answers.' "I'm home most nights and have security footage to prove it."

"That's convenient," one cop said.

"Isn't it?" I smiled at him.

"Were you at home last night?" Cop One asked.

"My husband and I had dinner with friends down the hall, then went home."

"What's this about?" Cruz demanded.

"Daniel Stone was found dead on the beach, just down from where Mrs. Thornton lives. Convenient, don't you think?" Cop Two said.

Murder on our beach? What was Daniel doing there? "The building has numerous security cameras, and they all work," I said, struggling to control my shock.

The first cop handed a paper to Cruz, which he perused. "They're going to take possession of the tapes," he said.

"Do you want the number for our security person, who can walk your guys through the process?" I asked.

"You better not be talking about Avery English," Cruz whispered in my ear. I nodded. He rolled his eyes. "Give them Seven's number. He'd kill me if I got her involved any more than she already is."

Cruz and Seven had been friends since… they were vague on the details. Though each man made it clear they had the other's back.

I was beginning to think that the meeting was

finally over and I'd be dismissed. Wrong. They had me start from the beginning and go over the same ground, asking basically the same questions, though worded a bit differently. I longed to run out, grab Pryce, and go home for a walk on the beach. Would it be the same after all the violence?

Cruz finally cut them off. "My client's tired, and if you're planning to ask the same questions a third time, how about a break first?"

"If we have any further questions…"

"I'll make her available," Cruz said.

"Don't leave town," Cop Two said.

I followed Cruz out. We met Pryce in the lobby, and he hugged me.

"Do you think I'm really a suspect in Daniel's murder?" I asked Cruz.

"What?" Pryce snapped.

"Sorry, I hadn't received news of that before we got here or I'd have told you," Cruz said. "What I think is that they're looking at everyone. Your security footage will corroborate your story, and that of your witnesses, that you were home last night, and that will be the end of their interest in you."

"I wanted Daniel in jail, not dead," I said.

Cruz's phone dinged; he took it out and read the screen. "Don't worry, you've got the best on your side." He patted my shoulder and took off at a fast clip.

Pryce hooked his arm around me, and we

walked back to the car.

"If I'm arrested for something I didn't do, are you going to come visit me?"

"I'm going to do you one better and spirit you out of the country to somewhere with no extradition."

"Beachy and warm, please."

"You got it." Pryce brushed a kiss on my cheek.

Chapter Thirty-Four

A quiet couple of weeks passed, Pryce and I staying close to home with the occasional trek down to the beach, which wasn't as much fun since we were constantly looking over our shoulders. Floyd had to move on to another assignment; we couldn't keep him around for security indefinitely, and with Daniel dead, we couldn't be sure it was even necessary.

Seven stayed in touch with his friend on the force and found out that I was no longer a suspect in Daniel's murder, since my alibi checked out, the security tapes showing me to be where I said I'd been. Daniel's body had been found down at the other end of the beach, rather than in our backyard as the cops suggested. A woman had been seen leaving the area where his body was found, but they hadn't been able to identify her. She was currently not a person of interest, just someone they wanted to talk to.

Finally, declaring that we needed an evening out, Harper found a seafood restaurant that had opened recently to rave reviews and made reservations for the six of us. After a fun dinner with friends, we walked out of the restaurant to find that the sky had deepened and sparkled with stars. I hadn't wanted to go, but I was happy that we did.

Traffic was lighter than usual as we headed home. One moment, we were the only car in the intersection, and the next, another car rolled up alongside us, honking insistently. I powered down the window and looked over at them. The driver was masked and staring at us as we stared down the barrel of a gun. I hit the gas. The back window shattered.

"Hit it," Pryce barked, pulling out his phone and calling 911.

Tires screeched on pavement. I glanced in the rearview mirror to see that the sedan had fallen back but was now rapidly gaining and, after cutting off another car, rolled up on our bumper.

My hands gripped the steering wheel tightly. Never had I driven so recklessly before, weaving in and out of traffic. I swerved back and forth, not taking my eyes off the road. The sedan attempted to slip between me and a car going the opposite direction, which honked furiously.

"What do I do?" I screeched.

"You're doing great, babe." Pryce had turned and was staring out the shattered back window.

The sedan sped up and attempted to get around me. I jerked the wheel, turning onto a side street. "Lost them." I breathed a huge sigh, my hands shaking.

"You okay?" Pryce leaned over and kissed my

cheek. "We need to get out of here before they come back."

I agreed and sped up. "I hope the cops get here quickly."

But at the next corner, the sedan reappeared, turning in front of my car and coming at us head-on. I gripped the wheel so hard, I thought my fingers would snap. I turned hard to avoid the oncoming headlights. The sedan plowed into the driver's side, and the airbags deployed, making me see stars.

Pryce had stayed on the line with 911 and now reported being struck, telling the operator, "Where the hell are the cops? We've been shot at and now slammed into."

"We need to get out of here." I shook my head, hoping to diminish the ringing in my ears.

"Sorry. Just please hurry." Pryce ended the call. "We need to get out. The other driver is still inside; we can make a run for it."

"It's all residential here, and I don't want to bring trouble to someone's door. What if there are kids?" I shuddered.

"We'll figure it out." Pryce shoved his door open.

I groaned, sure I'd have bruises, as he helped me climb over the seat, and his arms encircled my waist as he lifted me out and set me on the sidewalk.

"We're going to have to run." He looked down at my heels, and I kicked them off, thankful for the smooth pavement under my feet. He grabbed my hand, but we didn't get more than a couple of steps before the driver of the sedan stepped in front of us, waving a gun in one hand, the other clutching her head. Unsteady on her feet but managing somehow to stay upright, she stalked toward us, closing the distance with her chin lifted in a challenge.

"You bitches…" The gun wavered wildly back and forth, barely under control.

"Meet Daniel Stone's second wife," I said, recognizing her more from the picture Avery had sent over than our unpleasant encounter at the restaurant.

"Amy Peters," Pryce said in disgust. "I'm sure we can work something out where you don't end up in jail."

"Please," Amy sneered. "I've stayed out of jail this long." Her eyes blazed with anger as she marched towards us.

Pryce's arm shot out, giving me a hard shove, and he stepped in front of me.

"We're in this together," I said, moving to stand at his shoulder. "Why are you doing this? I can't come up with a single thing we've ever done to you." I moved closer to Pryce as she paced forward.

"What the hell haven't you done?" Amy spit. "Hold still, you two. I'm in charge here. I've only got a couple of bullets, and I'd hate to only kill one of you. That's all the guy that sold it to me had. Tried to buy one from a gun shop, but my application got rejected, so I thought going back for ammo would be a red flag."

The porch light of a neighboring house flicked on. Then I heard what sounded like a door closing, and the light went back off. I hoped whoever it was had gone straight for a phone to call the cops.

Amy swung her gun around in a wild arc. "You two are clueless," she screamed, her voice echoed in the night air.

Does she even know how to use a firearm? From the way her hand's shaking, I have to wonder.

Amy started singing as she took a step closer, the words unintelligible, her eyes flitting between me and Pryce. "I couldn't have asked for a better scenario, the two of you here together. I'm liking this turn of events. It's as though the universe was listening."

"Don't you want the satisfaction of telling us why you want us dead?" *Keep her talking*, I thought. *Give the cops time to show up.* "We never did anything to you," I said again.

"Liar, liar," she seethed.

"Telling us what we did is the least you can do before you kill us." Pryce leveled an assessing stare at her. "Tell me. I'd really like to know why." As he continued to talk, his tone turned less demanding, more placating.

"Do you know what it's like, finding out your husband is married to another woman? Lili was *so* perfect, except she whored herself all over town. And Daniel fawned all over her." Amy let out a shriek that echoed down the quiet street. "Couldn't believe my luck when you were arrested for the murder." She smirked at Pryce. "Lili never wanted to marry you; she just wanted your money. I got a good laugh when you were charged for my crime. I lured her to the boatyard—I'd worked there once and knew there were plenty of places to hide a body. Just a bonus that I got lucky in choosing a boat that you once owned. As far as I was concerned, best possible scenario. Then the charges got dropped. What the hell happened there?" she raged. "How is it that you're not in jail? No need to worry about that now." She chuckled, an unsettling sound.

"You're mad at me because I didn't stand trial for a murder I didn't commit... That explains your jones for me, sort of, but why Rella?"

"You're not very smart. Because I don't want to go to jail. Now I just need to pin Daniel's death on one of you so I don't have to worry about the cops showing up at my RV in the Everglades. Can't have them ruining my peace and quiet."

It was beautiful in the Glades, but live there...? I shuddered.

"Why kill your husband?" Pryce asked.

"Last thing I needed was for Daniel to turn a suspicious eye my way." Amy started grumbling under her breath, "Daniel" being the only intelligible word in her mumblings. "Surprised you didn't do it yourself. But then, maybe you didn't know that he and your wife were meeting at a seedy motel. Must suck—two women, and neither one faithful."

"Daniel kidnapped me and dragged me to the motel," I told her. "I wasn't interested in him."

Amy continued as though she hadn't heard a word. "The last straw for me. After that night, he was angry, and there was no talking him down. He'd always had a temper and slapped me around a few times, but after Lili's death, he beat me good. I might've forgiven him, even though I couldn't get out of bed for days, but then he gloated that he'd never laid a finger on her." Pain was etched on her face as she recalled what'd happened. "After that, I swore never again, and always had a knife on me."

"Why not just leave him and start a new life?" I listened for sirens, hoping they'd make it in time.

"I wasn't ready for it to be over." *Duh* in Amy's tone.

"How did he end up dead, then?" Pryce asked.

"It was one of those spontaneous things. Daniel had a business investment to check on, or so he claimed, and I insisted on going along. As we walked on the beach, he was going on about a big payday the whole time. Said he'd made mistakes, but not a second time, he swore. When I tried to get him to tell me what he was talking about, he turned on me. The look on his face scared me. I stepped back, but he punched me twice. I pulled my knife and stabbed him in the throat. The look of surprise…" She smiled.

I molded myself to Pryce.

"As though I was going to take it," Amy continued. "I'd warned him—no more—but he didn't believe me. There was blood everywhere." She grimaced. "I had to get it out of my clothes, so I grabbed the knife and ran into the water, then doubled back to the car, hoping it would take a few days to find him. Forgot it was a popular beach, and it only took a couple of hours. Realized my mistake on the way home and raced inside, grabbed his money from where he stashed it, along with a few of my belongings, and lit out with plans to fly under the radar. Be someone new. Go make a new life. Haven't decided on a name yet. It'll come to me."

"I'll give you more money, and you can go start that life right now," Pryce said.

"I believe in getting even. Same thing I told Lili. I told Daniel no more hookups; I wasn't going to tolerate it." Amy spit out her contempt. "I'm tired of talking. Getting parched." Her eyes not quite focused, she slithered forward. "Say good-bye, you two."

Finally, sirens could be heard in the distance, but how long would it take for them to get here?

"You mind if we have a moment?" Pryce asked.

"Go ahead." She wiped her face with the back of her hand, which she scrubbed off on her clothes.

Pryce turned towards me and put his arms around me, whispering, "I'm going to jump her, and you're going to run."

"If she pulls the trigger..." I shuddered. "I don't want you getting hurt, or worse. You're barely recovered from the last attack."

"Love you."

"Love you back."

"Enough already," Amy yelled. "Say good-bye."

"On three." Pryce had lowered his voice still further. "She can't shoot us both at the same time, and I'm going to try to tackle her." He turned, not taking his eyes off her. "Three." He pushed me away and launched himself at Amy.

The gun went off.

I screamed.

Pryce wrestled the gun away and kicked it into a nearby bush, shoving Amy onto her butt. In one move, she leapt to her feet, knife in hand, jabbing at Pryce.

I let out a blood-curdling scream, which startled her. Pryce jumped forward and managed a side-kick to her knee. She tumbled to the ground, still clutching the knife, which he kicked out of her hand. She screamed.

Two cop cars came at us from different directions, lights flashing, laying rubber as they came to a stop. They were out of their cars in an instant, guns drawn. "Hands in the air," one shouted.

"I really could use a martini to calm my nerves," I said, knowing only Pryce could hear.

"You're on."

Chapter Thirty-Five

Pryce and I did as we were told.

Amy, groaning and clutching at her knee, got back on her feet and ran. Despite shouts to stop, she didn't break stride and disappeared up the street, a cop in hot pursuit. It wouldn't surprise me to hear that she was on the track team in school.

We were questioned, and from the cop's incredulous look, he didn't believe our story. Even to my ears, it sounded farfetched. He did let me call Cruz, looking surprised when I mentioned his name. An answering service picked up—better than voicemail, I guessed, but I figured we were on our own.

The second cop came back empty-handed. It wasn't long before more backup arrived, including a K-9 unit.

We were loaded into the back of a cop car and taken to the station. I'd vowed not to return, and here we were. The cop assured me that my car was headed to impound and would be available for pickup once released.

It surprised me to find Cruz waiting for us at the station, griping that he didn't get dessert.

"What's your favorite?" I asked.

"Crème brûlée."

I licked my lips at his response and made a mental note to see that several were delivered to his office.

"I don't suppose you can represent us both?" Pryce asked.

"Are they under arrest?" Cruz asked the cop, who came and stood in front of us.

"Not yet." He motioned for us to follow him.

I was shown into a room to cool my heels, and I assumed Pryce was taken to another, since the door closed before I could see where they went.

It wasn't long before another cop showed up, Cruz at his side. They both sat across the table from me, and I noted that the cop didn't read me my rights. "Sounds like you had a busy night."

I unleashed a brittle laugh and rubbed my eyes. "We tried out a new restaurant, had this amazing dinner, and were driving home, hugging the water as much as the road allowed, when…" I went on to tell them what happened.

He asked question after question, and I kept Cruz's admonitions in the back of my mind: *short and sweet*, close enough anyway. As expected, he had me go over the night's events several times.

"Did this Amy Peters confess to murdering Liliana Ford?" the cop asked.

"Amy bragged about luring Lili to the boatyard. She had a hate-on for Lili, as they were married to the same man. Having met him, I didn't see the attraction." I shook my head. "And she confessed to stabbing Daniel."

More questions, all of which I answered, making it clear whenever I didn't know something.

"Wait here while I question your husband." The cop stood and moved to the door.

Cruz stood, leaning down and whispering, "You did a good job." He patted me on the back, and then the door closed on the two.

I crossed my arms on the table and laid my head on them, closing my eyes and talking myself into a state of relaxation. There wasn't a clock, so it was hard to know how much time went by. Long enough for me to doze off and wake with a crick in my neck.

Finally, the door opened, and Cruz and Pryce stood on the threshold.

"You're free to go." Cruz smiled.

Pryce moved closer, holding out his hand, and I stood.

"Where's Amy Peters?" I asked.

"Under arrest," Cruz said. "Slick thing eluded the police and managed to sneak into someone's backyard. It took the K-9 unit to sniff her out. She punched him in the nose, and he bit her."

"Too bad he didn't eat her hand," I said with no sympathy.

"You two are perfect for each other—Pryce said something similar." Cruz grinned. "Another charge will be leveled for abusing the dog."

"What about the murders?" Pryce asked.

"First thing after being read her rights, she requested an attorney. She's going to need a good one if murder one charges are filed. It won't be me," Cruz said.

"If she makes bail, someone will let us know?" Pryce asked.

"Amy isn't going anywhere," Cruz said. "She'll be a guest of the state for the rest of her life."

"Let's get out of here." Pryce motioned.

"We don't have a ride," I said.

"Oh yes we do. Cruz called Seven, and he's cooling his heels in the reception area." Pryce and Cruz shook hands.

I threw my arms around Cruz in a hard hug. "You're the best. Just like your billboards say."

He laughed, and the three of us walked out together.

Chapter Thirty-Six

A couple of weeks of peace and quiet passed without us having to look over our shoulders. In that time, Amy Peters was charged with two counts of first-degree murder and denied bail. They also tacked on an arson charge, which I took to mean she was the one who started the fire in Olive and Millie's condo. She wouldn't be getting out of prison ever.

One morning, Harper called, issuing an edict that Pryce and I come down the hall for morning coffee.

"I wonder what she's up to now," I said, ending the call, then told Pryce about being ordered not to waste time.

"No clue." Pryce laughed. "At least we're dressed."

"I've never wanted a ratty old robe more than I do now. The shock on their faces would be fun."

"They'd blame me for being a bad influence." He pulled me to my feet, slung his arm around me, and we went out the door and down the hall.

Knowing Harper was expecting us and the door would be unlocked, I opened it with a half-hearted knock. In the entry, I yelled, "We're here."

"Took you long enough," Harper yelled from the kitchen.

Pryce rolled his eyes, shaking his head.

I took his hand and led him into the kitchen, where our friends were seated around the island. We claimed seats in front of two empty mugs, and Grey filled them up.

Pryce shot Grey and Seven a *What's up?* look, and they responded with smirks.

"So what's new?" Avery asked.

"I think that's what we're here to find out," I said, knowing from her smug look that she knew.

Harper slid off her stool. "We asked you to come over so we could share our big news." She motioned for Avery to stand.

"Huge announcement." Avery threw her arms wide.

"You two have cooked something up, and this is the first I'm hearing about it? Not even in on the planning?" I did my best to tamp down my hurt feelings at being left out.

"Do Grey and Seven know what you two are up to?" Pryce left off "this time," but it was clearly heard by all.

"We're eloping to Las Vegas," Harper announced. She and Avery flicked their ring fingers in the air.

"Congrats." I clapped. The marriage

announcement didn't surprise me, but Las Vegas definitely did. "There's no beach there. Hoover Dam, but that's not the same." *Is it?* I telegraphed to Pryce, who laughed.

"Congratulations." He shook hands with Grey and Seven.

"I'm a lucky man." Seven pulled Avery into his arms.

Grey winked at Harper.

"You're going to have a dual role," Avery said to me. "Flower girl/maid of honor chick." Ta-da in her tone. "And Pryce: best dude."

"When's the big day?" he asked.

"Two weeks," Grey said. "We've all got clients to square away before we can leave town for a few days."

"When are you planning to break the happy news to the rest of the family?" I covered my grimace. Gram was going to be devastated when she found out she missed the ceremony.

"When we get back, we're going to have a big party," Harper said.

"Just want all of you to know that I'll say something nice at your funerals," I said to a chorus of groans. "Gram will kill Harper first, then Avery. She'll probably spare the guys. With Harper's dad, it'll probably be the other way around. Avery's family is a little more chill."

"Gram will understand when I explain it to her," Harper said.

There must be vodka in her coffee.

"If you need me to do anything, I'm more than happy," I offered.

It turned out that Grey and Harper had been talking about tying the knot, so he bought a ring and they made it official. When Seven heard the news, he decided to see if he could reel his woman in, and after he calmed all Avery's insecurities, she said yes.

"Before you think we left you out of the planning..." Avery said. "We just said yes two nights ago, and the guys got together and made all the arrangements."

"Let's plan a shopping day and lunch," I said. "Give me a date, and I'll put together something special."

Chapter Thirty-Seven

The phone rang early, which was never a good sign. Pryce grabbed my phone. Glancing at the screen, he half-laughed. "You're not going to want to take this call. My advice — get it over with; she'll just call back."

It was too early for drama. I took my phone from his outstretched hand and groaned at the screen. It stopped ringing. And started again. At least Pryce didn't say, "Told you so."

The third time it started up, I answered it. "Good morning, Gram. You're up early," I said with more cheerfulness than I felt.

"I need you to super swear that you won't tell anyone about this phone call," Gram rasped.

I'd bet she'd just woken up herself. "Too late for that. My hub is lying right here and knows it's you."

"You need to wrestle the same promise out of him."

"I swear for both of us. Tell me you're not in any kind of trouble."

"Not yet. But it's hovering." Gram coughed. "Meet me for lunch. It can't be any place we've gone before, and we can't be seen. Absolutely no word to you-know-who. Either of them."

"You're scaring me," I said.

"None of that," she tsked. "You and me need to get our noggins together and get this little dilemma worked out."

"I know the perfect place and will text you the address," I said.

"You're a honey. We want to beat the lunch rush."

I didn't tell her no need to worry about that. We decided on a time and hung up, and I scrolled through my phone, found the address I was looking for, and sent her a text.

"When Gram asks why you brought me, tell her you couldn't shake me. I have no intention of missing out on whatever's going down."

"Is it possible that she knows about the wedding?" My brows went up.

"Knowing Gram, if she did know, she'd be banging on Harper's door," Pryce assured me. "And if that happened, Harper would have had to tell her everything and they would've worked it out. I'm thinking a promise to take over Morningside for the biggest party of all time might mollify her."

Pryce and I got up and took our coffee and laptops outside to deal with several work issues.

Checking the time, I jumped up and ran down the hall to shower and change into an a-line t-shirt dress and a pair of sandals. I grabbed my purse and met Pryce, who'd also changed, in the hall.

As often as I could, I opted for a route that kept us along the water. Today, traffic was light, and it didn't take long to get to the rundown blue-and-red building I'd chosen for lunch. The little shack specialized in tacos, and there were a handful of other things on the one-page menu, but I'd never explored.

Pryce laughed. "Gram's got a great car." He eyed the red '57 Thunderbird. "Doesn't she worry every time she gets out that it won't be there when she returns?"

"Besides an alarm, she uses a steering wheel lock and doesn't generally leave it unattended for long. So far, it hasn't been boosted."

"Wonder where she is?" We'd gotten out, and he looked around. Only one table on the outside patio was occupied.

"We'll find her inside, chatting it up with someone." And that's where we found her, sitting at the bar and laughing with the bartender.

"Did you card this woman?" I asked in a demanding tone that had both the bartender and Gram laughing harder. "We're going to sit outside." I picked up her beer and steered her towards the door; the inside was too dark and oppressive.

Pryce stayed behind to place an order for food and drinks while Gram and I claimed a table outside, sitting across from one another under the big umbrella.

"Thank you for agreeing to meet on such short notice," she said.

"Never worry about calling me, no matter the time; I'd rearrange my schedule if necessary," I reassured her.

Pryce came out, drinks in hand, and set a margarita in front of me. Like Gram, he'd ordered a beer. "We've got your back." He toasted.

Gram took a deep breath. "I did something, and then something else, and now I need you to make it all work. Happy ending, that sort of thing."

I groaned inwardly, doubting that I'd like where this conversation was going. "I mean this in the nicest way — what are you talking about?"

"I overheard a conversation between Harper and Grey and know that they're eloping to Las Vegas of all places." Gram sniffed. "I'm not certain whose idea it was, but it's a terrible one."

I was surprised Harper would even mention the E-word with Gram in hearing range.

"How is it that you heard this conversation, and do they know?" Pryce stared her down.

Gram shook her head. "You can't tell them this next part, you just can't."

I patted her hand. "Just tell us."

"I heard Avery ordering cool spy stuff on the phone. I mean, she did it right in front of me, so it wasn't eavesdropping." Gram nodded, agreeing with herself. "When I got home, I decided to check out the website, and the next thing I knew, I'd ordered a few items of my own. One was a listening device."

Pryce nudged me under the table.

"What good is having such a device if you're not going to test it out, make sure the thing works? So I put it in Harper's living room. Makes sense, don't you think? I mean, better than the bedroom. Though there was this one part that I had to mute fast." Gram's cheeks flamed.

My mouth made an "O" shape as my cheeks burned at what she was insinuating.

"You're telling us that at some point during the recordings you made, you heard the impending nuptials being discussed?" Pryce could barely control his grin.

Gram nodded. "I wanted to march right over and pull Harper's hair out. Did she think for one second that I wouldn't want to be there for her wedding? Didn't she know I'd be crushed not to be?"

I winced, having known this would be her reaction.

"I couldn't wallow, as I had plans of my own to make and a short time to pull them off," she continued. "If those two want an Elvis impersonator, I can make that happen here. Though Jimmy Buffet would be more appropriate."

"What exactly have you done?" I asked, even though I didn't want to know. Or did I?

"Well, uh…" Gram drained her beer. "I'll take another one," she shouted, waving the empty bottle at the server.

"You're driving," I reminded her in a stern tone.

"Two's my limit." Gram held up her fingers.

"Where were we?" I asked.

"Gram was just about to finish outing herself and share all the sneaking around she's been doing," Pryce said with a grin. "I'm betting it's something big."

Gram's cheeks pinkened. "Since I also overheard them making all their reservations and such in Vegas, I was able to cancel everything," she said in a rush, shushing us before barreling on. "Think big blowout." She waved her arms around. "I've got everything planned. Ceremony on the beach. An after bash by the pool. I've reserved the entire area. Who can bring a party better than me? No one."

How could she have pulled that off without the engaged couples finding out? I'd winced several times as Gram laid out what she'd done and her plans. "You're going to have four people fighting over who gets to do you bodily harm first. The only thing that might save your backside is…" I couldn't think of anything.

"They might go easier on her because she's older and, more importantly, they love her,"

Pryce reminded me.

"Gram—"

"I don't like that tone of voice."

Pryce patted my hand. "What is it you want from us?" At Gram's raised eyebrows, he said, "Yes, us. I'm not feeding my wife to the wolves. Nor am I letting anyone else do it."

"It's just that Rella's a problem-solver and does it all day, every day. Don't you, dear?" Gram gave me a toothy smile.

Thank goodness the food arrived just then. I was going to be mad if I found I could only pick at it. Thankfully, that didn't happen, and a full stomach makes me less grouchy.

Once the dishes were cleared away, I nudged Pryce a couple of times, hoping he could decipher that to mean, *You question the heck out of her*.

"What do you want us to do?" Pryce asked. "We're a team, so you get both of us."

"I've reserved a hotel room down at the beach not far from where the ceremony will take place. All Rella has to do is get the girls to show up. I've arranged for them to have their hair and makeup done there. As for you…" Gram nodded at Pryce. "I was wondering how to get the guys corralled, and that can be your job. I made it easier by also booking them a room."

How was I supposed to do that? They'd see through any lies. "Aren't there a few more details that are going to be impossible to bring together without their knowledge? Their dresses for one?"

"Got that covered." Gram tapped her temple. "When they're not home—and you'll have better knowledge of when that would be than me—you get into their closets and grab the dresses. Also figure out what the guys are wearing and grab that too."

I eeped. Not for the first time in the conversation, I found myself wishing I hadn't answered the phone.

"I'd do it, but you're best friends and will know when's a good time," Gram reasoned. "I don't have the nerves for breaking in again anyway. I'm not cut out for too much sneaking around. What if I get caught?"

I laughed, or maybe it was a snort. Now she reaches her nerve limit?

Pryce squeezed my hand, knowing I was about to explode, having long ago surpassed the limits of what I would agree to do.

"This will take some time to plan, and the wedding they arranged is in two weeks," Pryce said in a more conciliatory tone than I was feeling.

"Too late for dragging your feet, the invitations are being hand-delivered today." Gram returned his fierce stare, not flinching.

You're out of your mind. For once, I wanted to blurt out what I was thinking, not struggle to think of something nice. "You need to call a family meeting, fess up to cancelling their plans, and tell them they have to go for yours." I'd long ago drained my margarita and was licking my lips for more.

"How did you cancel the Las Vegas plans?" Pryce asked.

"I may have overheard the name of the wedding chapel and the hotel, and it was easy to pretend to be Grey's assistant."

"He's going to get a cancellation confirmation," I told her. *Then what?*

"That's why I called Rella. She fixes problems all day long, and this one should be easy."

I turned my glass upside down in case I'd missed a drop.

Pryce chuckled. "Here's what we're going to do… We've got a few days to come up with a plan of some kind, and that comes with a big maybe. Know that if certain cancellations come to light, this could blow up at any moment, and the only way out is nothing but the truth."

Gram huffed. "You can do better than that."

"The reality is… maybe not. And I'd like your promise not to get all attitudinal if the you-know-what hits the fan and it all goes south." Pryce held out his hand. Gram made several faces before extending her hand. The two shook.

Pryce paid the bill, and we walked out to the parking lot together. He nodded toward the car, and I took the hint. I engulfed Gram in a hug. "When you ask for a favor, it's a doozie." I left the two to have what appeared to be an intense chat.

"Great, now I have a stomachache," I mumbled to myself as I slid into the passenger seat. I stuck the key in the ignition, turned on the air, and reclined the seat.

It was several minutes before Pryce slid behind the wheel. "You okay?"

I groaned. "What the heck am I supposed to do about any of this?"

"Gram's something all right. I had a firm chat with her and told her that in all likelihood, the truth will have to come out to pull off what she wants. No way will I let it interfere with your friendship with Harper and Avery."

"If I even try to go through with this con job, so much for being besties. And for one of the biggest events of their lives. I should've womanned up and told her, 'You're on your own.'"

"You're not to worry your beautiful head, wifey. I've got a trick or two up my sleeve."

"There goes your friendships with Grey and Seven."

"I promise nothing that drastic is going to happen."

Chapter Thirty-Eight

The next morning was the guys' usual morning to work out, and as usual, one or the other pounded on the door on the way to the elevator. Pryce was ready. He threw open the door and looked down the hallway, making sure that the coast was clear as Grey and Seven watched with bemused expressions.

"Get the heck in here," Pryce hissed, "before one of your almost-wives sees that you've detoured."

"What's going on?"

Pryce held the door open and pointed to the kitchen, closing it behind them. "There's coffee, and you're going to need it."

I waved when they walked in and slid onto stools, then set mugs down in front of them and filled them with freshly brewed coffee. Pie would have been good, but I didn't have any.

"Do I swear them to secrecy like we had to?" Pryce asked me.

"This is your party. I'm going to pretend this is the first I'm hearing what you're about to tell them." I flashed him a nervous smile.

Both Grey and Seven looked at him wide-eyed, *Well?* on their faces.

"I suppose the beginning would be a good place to start," Pryce teased.

"Spit it out," Seven said.

"Gram called…"

Grey and Seven groaned.

Pryce smirked at them. "I waylaid you this morning with the hope that we can make everyone happy and all stay friends." He went on to relay the conversation with Gram pretty much word for word.

Grey nodded as he listened. "A cancellation confirmation popped up in my email this morning, and figuring it was a mistake, I planned to investigate when I got to the office. Now, no need."

"Rewind to the beginning," Seven huffed. "You're telling us that Gram put a bug in Grey and Harper's living room? Is it still there?"

"Didn't think to ask that question, but it's Gram, so probably." Pryce chuckled.

"It won't be there long." Grey glared at the other two. "Though maybe I shouldn't be so hasty. Setting her up to listen to something that will scorch her ears would be quite satisfying."

I pursed my lips, trying not to laugh. *Too late.*

"We need to come up with a good plan for which I can take credit, thus maintaining the favorite-grandson-in-law spot." Pryce grinned.

I looked down, my shoulders shaking.

"The reason Harper suggested eloping to Las

Vegas is that she wanted a stress-free wedding, or as close as we could get, knowing Gram would pull out all the stops and throw a circus event." Grey finished off his coffee.

I stood and refilled the mugs.

"And Avery, who's ready to jump at any excitement, didn't hesitate, not having been there before being another plus for going all in. Though after thinking it over, she did begin worrying about how to tell her parents," Seven said.

"One of your options is to be in on the surprise. Get with Gram and make sure she doesn't go overboard," Pryce suggested. "If you plan to blow off her wedding plans altogether, then one or both of you needs to tell her. Know that she's already had invitations delivered, and you can bet she'll have you making the calls to cancel."

"You think this situation is so funny," Grey grumbled. "I'm surprised that she called you. What fixer experience do *you* have?"

I waved my hand. "Gram called me. After learning what she wanted, while I struggled for a nice way to tell her she was on her own, my amazing husband stepped up and took the pressure off me. Then assured both of us that he'd come up with a plan, even if it meant telling the truth." I smiled at him.

"Gram's an early riser. First thing tomorrow morning, we arrive at dawn and have a sit-down," Seven suggested. "Have her detail everything she's done to pull off this surprise wedding. Then we make it clear that there's been a change of leadership and we'll decide what happens next."

"When you leave, she'll be alive and well?" I asked.

"Maybe," Grey said.

Chapter Thirty-Nine

The guys met with Gram, and I didn't get one detail except that I was to get Harper and Avery to the hotel not far from where the wedding would take place. I planned a bridal shower for the night before, which would include spa activities, and the next day, stylists would arrive for hair and makeup and get them dressed. That we'd been able to keep all the frenzy that went into the planning from Harper and Avery was shocking.

Everything went smoothly until there was a knock on the door and the two stylists arrived, a large case in each hand. "Ready, ladies?"

"You're getting married," I told Harper and Avery.

The stylists watched in amusement. They knew what was going on but had obviously assumed I'd tell Harper and Avery ahead of time. They both shot questions at me, one after another, with no time in between to answer. Not that I was surprised.

"Sorry, no time for questions." I zipped my lips. "Don't you both love a surprise wedding?"

They shook their heads.

"I can't believe you." Harper sank down on the bed.

"Agree with you." Avery glanced at the door more than once.

No running, my friends. I straightened to my full height. "Listen up, you two," I barked. "You get into your damn dresses and do it now. You have no idea what's been going on behind the scenes. And when you do find out, it's going to be a great story for your kids." They didn't look convinced. "Up now." I motioned. "If you even think about dragging your freshly manicured toes, I'm going to stick my foot up your butts. Morphed into Gram there for a second." I grinned at myself. Their looks of shock spurred me on. "Get dressed." I pointed to the stylists, who were laughing. "They're waiting. Trust me, you're not going to want to miss a second."

Once they were dressed and ready, security guards from WD came to the door and escorted us down to the beach, where two golf carts festooned with lace bows and flowers awaited the brides on the sand. As a bridesmaid, I rode with the rest of the entourage in the second one. Having left earlier, the guys were already at the site.

A simple altar had been constructed on a platform of white sand, the backdrop of clear blue water reflecting the cloudless sky. The chairs on each side were for family only. This time, Gram had stuck to her word and made sure the couples would have their privacy. All the families were in attendance; Seven's and Grey's parents had even flown in. The million or so guests were for later, at the reception.

The music started up, and I walked up the boardwalk, dropping birdseed, to the platform at the end draped in white tulle and dotted with potted palms. I took in a deep breath, salty air filling my lungs, and winked at my husband, who blew me a kiss.

Harper and Avery walked up the aisle together in simple, elegant white gowns, their hair pinned up with small gardenias peeking out. Both looked absolutely gorgeous. Their radiant smiles were worth all the angst.

The minister stood, prepared to hear their vows, and the two couples lined up in front of him.

The vows passed in a blur, "I do" ending them, their words full of conviction.

"You may kiss the bride."

Both brides were bent back and given kisses that had everyone catcalling and whistling. They stood with big smiles, and waved back at everyone.

~*~

Other Titles by Deborah Brown

BISCAYNE BAY SERIES

PARADISE SERIES

Deborah's books are available on Amazon
amazon.com/Deborah-Brown/e/B0059MAIKQ

About the Author

Deborah Brown is an Amazon bestselling author of the Paradise series. She lives on the Gulf of Mexico, with her ungrateful animals, where Mother Nature takes out her bad attitude in the form of hurricanes.

For a free short story, sign up for my newsletter. It will also keep you up-to-date with new releases and special promotions:
www.deborahbrownbooks.com

Follow on FaceBook:
facebook.com/DeborahBrownAuthor

You can contact her at Wildcurls@hotmail.com

Deborah's books are available on Amazon

amazon.com/Deborah-Brown/e/B0059MAIKQ

Made in the USA
Las Vegas, NV
24 April 2025

21317331R00177